OMNIBOZ

Tales from The Land of Oz

Edited by **JENDIA GAMMON** and **ERNIE CHIARA**

ISBN: 978-1-967550-08-1 (trade paper)
ISBN: 978-1-967550-09-8 (hardcover)
ISBN: 978-1-967550-10-4 (ebook/ePub)
Library of Congress Catalog Number: 2026942090

First printing edition: May 15, 2026
Published by Stars and Sabers Publishing in the United States of America.
Cover art copyright © 2026 Eric Shanower. All rights reserved.
Cover Design and Layout: Dash Creative
Edited by Jendia Gammon and Ernie Chiara
Proofreading and Interior Layout by Scarlett R. Algee

Stars and Sabers Publishing is an imprint of Roaring Spring Productions, LLC.
Los Angeles, California

https://www.starsandsabers.com/

CONTENTS

OMNIBOZ

Tales from The Land of Oz

INTRODUCTION
Jendia Gammon

When I first read L. Frank Baum's Oz books as I child, I was more than transported to his various fairylands though his lens as a "Royal Historian of Oz." I was given a glimpse into the possibilities of invention, of camaraderie, and of wild imagination just when my growing mind needed it the most. Baum's fourteen original Oz books set the stage for me to create my own worlds and characters, and even through my science fiction, fantasy, and horror books and short stories, nods to Oz abound.

As I am now in the wondrous position of creating an anthology inspired by Baum's Oz books, I find this to be a full-circle moment. I've included my own story within these pages, emphasizing how even the smallest denizens of Oz can leave a big impression. I am delighted to have Ernie Chiara as my co-editor and fellow contributor, and renowned Oz veteran Eric Shanower as my cover artist and story contributor. I'm welcoming friends and former contributors Adrian Tchaikvosky, Helen Glynn Jones, Dennis K. Crosby, and Vincent V. Cava back into the fold. And I welcome Jeannie Warner, Patrick Barb, Nicole Field, and J.R. Dawson to Stars and Sabers. Each of their stories is powerfully unique. Some are lighthearted, and some are quite dark.

Thank you to Scarlett R. Algee for edits and Mike Trobiano of Dash Creative for design assistance. Thank you to Helen Glynn Jones for the wonderful idea of using the title *Omniboz*.

While this is *not* a children's book, the reminder that Baum made a universe of terrors and wonders can be found in each story. Gather your courage and cross the Deadly Desert with me, and embark on the ultimate journey in *Omniboz: Tales from the Land of Oz*.

THE VISITORS' RETURN
Eric Shanower

I know I'm not much to look at as a trophy head, hanging on the wall here in this back hallway of Ozma's royal palace in the Emerald City. With my bulbous nose. These clumsy antlers. Long billy-goat whiskers. Big, square, slightly yellowing teeth. But for a while, I had a body that could strike—well, if not respect, at least confusion into the stoutest of hearts.

You see, Ozma and several of her friends once cobbled a couple sofas together with some spare parts to form a big, ungainly contraption. Palm leaf wings on both sides. A broom tied on back for a tail. And my head stuck on the front. They called this thing the Gump, since I previously belonged to the native Oz species known as Gump, back when I was a respectable, full-bodied animal and not just a head. Anyway, Ozma brought the whole monstrously embarrassing conglomeration to life as a sort of flying machine, so that I could carry her and her friends through the air.

Then, for Ozma's first act of international diplomacy, she sent a group of us to visit the USA—to give us Oz folks a look at the great wonders and workings of America and to let the Americans get a look at us celebrated folks from the Land of Oz. So back in ought-four, I carried six of us—the Scarecrow, the Tin Woodman, Jack Pumpkinhead, the Wogglebug, the wooden Sawhorse, and me—away to the far-off USA.

For nearly eight months, I flew us all up, down, and around, visiting cities and countryside and everywhere in between. We saw fascinating, remarkable sights and met all sorts of interesting, eccentric people. Each week, the newspapers trumpeted our latest activities. Our visit was big news there.

But I was ashamed of my freakish body. Everywhere we went, people stared and pointed. From the moment we arrived in the USA, all I kept saying to everybody was, "I want to go home." No matter how much I urged, cajoled, and persuaded, my companions didn't agree. I nearly despaired. Would I ever see home again? Finally, though, they'd had enough of the USA and wanted to return to Oz. Even then, I feared we'd never get away.

Here's how it was. By April 1905, we'd taken the most luxurious suite on the second floor of an excellent Chicago hotel. No higher room would do, you see, because the hodge-podge body I was saddled with wouldn't fit through any stairway above the second floor, much less on the elevator.

We had a lovely time in Chicago, seeing the museums, the parks, the lake. Then, people began accosting us in public, asking us to magically grant their requests. We retreated in confusion to our hotel. Still they came, by ones and twos, then dozens; then a steady stream became an unending stampede. Crowds jammed the hotel lobby and overwhelmed the front desk. The police swept the throng out of the hotel. But a sea of people surrounded the building and refused to disperse.

You see, newspapers across the nation had begun to report that my companions from Oz used magical powers to help people. Now everyone in the country wanted a magical favor.

One morning, we gathered in the sitting room of our hotel suite to discuss our situation. The others agreed the time had come to return to the Land of Oz. They'd grown homesick at long last. I had little to contribute but my usual refrain, "Let's go home."

The Scarecrow patted the arm of one of my sofas with his padded glove. "Even if we could escape the crowd outside, the Wogglebug is still missing."

The Sawhorse rolled his knot eyes. "Weeks without word from that overgrown insect—you'd think he'd at least let us know where he's gone."

"Maybe he went home without us," I said. "Let's go there and see."

The Tin Woodman paused in polishing his tin legs with a chamois rag. "I know the Wogglebug sometimes annoys us with his unfortunate habit of telling poor jokes, yet his store of knowledge has proven him an invaluable member of our party. We can't show up back in Oz without him."

We heard a roar from the crowd in the street outside.

"What's the commotion this time?" asked Jack Pumpkinhead.

From behind a window curtain, the Scarecrow peeked down at the street. We had to be careful near windows, you see, since the crowd below fell to screaming rabidly whenever they spotted one of us.

"Why, the Wogglebug's out there," said the Scarecrow. "I'm glad to see he hasn't fallen victim to some overeager exterminator, as I'd feared."

The Tin Woodman approached the other window. "I fear he'll fall victim to that crowd before he can reach the lobby."

As the Wogglebug struggled through the crowd, hands from every direction grasped at the poor enlarged insect, clawing him, tearing his clothes. Just when it appeared he'd lost the struggle and was sinking beneath the crowd, his wings flew open, pushing people aside. He leaped into the air. The Wogglebug's wings aren't powerful enough for true flight, but he swooped over the crowd and glided toward the front door of the hotel.

"I can't see him any longer," said the Scarecrow. "I hope he made it inside."

Presently a knock sounded on the suite door.

Jack Pumpkinhead, who was nearest, called, "Who is it?"

Weak tones trembled beyond the door. "It is I, Mr. H. M. Wogglebug, T. E., torn and forlorn. Please let me in."

Jack turned the lock and opened the door. I can't remember seeing a more bedraggled figure than the Wogglebug. What remained of his usual spotless clothing hung in rags; his posture sagged, his antennae drooped, and three of his four arms dragged the carpet.

"Come in quick, so Jack can shut the door," said the Sawhorse, "and lock it behind you."

The Wogglebug tottered into the room. His fourth hand held high a strip of fabric bright with dazzling colors. It looked like an unknotted necktie. He stared at it with an expression of intense admiration.

"Welcome back," said the Scarecrow. "Where have you been?"

"Ah," sighed the Wogglebug. "My friends, I have been at great pains to obtain my one and only love. This fabric of Wagnerian plaids, in the form of a lady's dress on a department store mannequin, captured my undying affection."

"You fell in love with a dress dummy?" asked the Tin Woodman.

"Not the dummy," said the Wogglebug. "The dress itself. Just look at this delightful pattern of artfully arranged checks. How my buggy heart sings!"

"I don't hear any singing," said Jack Pumpkinhead.

The Wogglebug cast a scornful look at Jack and continued. "The dress escaped my grasp. I pursued, helpless yet hopeful. I can hardly relate the many experiences I endured, which reduced my love to this final scrap. But at last, I clasped my darling to my breast, safe in my possession." He pressed the piece of fabric to the front of his carapace as he closed his eyes in what looked like rapture.

"As soon as you've recovered in a change of clothes," said the Scarecrow, "I suppose you'll grace us with a lengthy recitation of your adventures."

The Wogglebug looped the gaudy cloth around his neck. "Friends, the pursuit took me halfway across the globe. But to my surprise, the most challenging danger I faced occurred but minutes ago, before this very hotel. The mass of humanity outside seemed intent on detaining me to the point of obliteration."

"They've been out there for days now," said the Tin Woodman. "We daren't leave the hotel."

The Wogglebug's antennae curled. "What could account for such outrageous behavior?"

The Scarecrow's straw stuffing crinkled as he shrugged. "All those people think magic can solve their problems, and they want us to perform that magic for them. I went out at first to explain that we've used up the few wishes and magical notions we brought from Oz for emergencies. But they grabbed me and tugged me until they pulled me apart. I would have been lost if the Tin Woodman hadn't charged into the crowd, whirling his axe until the people fell back. He gathered all my pieces and rushed up to this suite, where the others put me back together. Half my straw was lost, so I'm a little flimsy until I find more."

"We wouldn't be in this fix," said the Sawhorse, "if the rest of you hadn't been silly enough to use magic in the first place. You, Scarecrow, whipping up automobiles for children too young to drive. Jack replacing wooden legs with real limbs of flesh. The Wogglebug providing magic lozenges to that Jubb family. And the Tin Woodman going off to distribute wishes to juvenile delinquents. Showoffs! You should be ashamed of yourselves."

"Wait a minute," said the Tin Woodman to the Sawhorse, "how did you find out about—"

"I read the papers like anyone," said the Sawhorse. "I may have sawdust for brains, but I'm not just a woodenhead, you know."

Jack tapped the side of his pumpkin head. "A seed of thought tells me our situation is the fault of that writer Baum and that illustrator MacDougall. They follow us around and report everything we do."

"We haven't seen them for weeks," said the Scarecrow.

"I believe they've been tracking me alone," said the Wogglebug. "I'm certain I sighted that Baum fellow several times in the distance as I pursued my beloved fabric."

"Then you needn't relate your adventures to us," said the Tin Woodman. "We'll read all about them in due time."

"That crowd shocked me," said the Wogglebug. "I suppose that no one badgered me for magic during my travels because newspapers in the curious lands I visited don't print news from the USA."

"Can we go home now?" I asked, hoping to turn the conversation to a more pressing matter. "The Wogglebug is back. Let's leave this foreign country and its crowds behind forever."

"The problem is how to leave," said the Scarecrow.

"Just the way we came," said Jack Pumpkinhead. "In the Gump."

"To be sure," said the Scarecrow. "But how will the Gump take flight? It's too big to fly out a window. If we go down to the street, that crowd will likely seize the Gump's palm leaf wings and thus destroy them. The rest of us will be lucky to escape intact."

"How about the roof of the hotel?" said the Tin Woodman. "When we first built the Gump, it took off with ease from the roof of the emerald palace. A similar strategy seems the answer."

The Scarecrow held up one flimsy finger. "But the Gump is too large to fit up the stairways."

The Wogglebug seemed a little recovered from his ordeal among the crowd. "We must disassemble the Gump and carry each piece up to the roof separately," he said. "Once there, we may reassemble him and fly away at our leisure."

I didn't like the idea of being taken apart before we reached home, lest some accident occur. But the risk seemed small, and I longed to return to Oz. I agreed to the plan. It seemed the only answer.

While the Wogglebug changed into his remaining suit of clothing and the Tin Woodman went down to the lobby to inform the front desk of our departure, the others packed our belongings into a small crate that the hotel janitor, at our summons, brought up from the basement. These belongings consisted of trinkets we'd acquired in our travels around the USA—small pot-metal reproductions of famous buildings and monuments, a photograph signed by the celebrated actors Fred Stone and David Montgomery, a scrapbook of newspaper clippings detailing our doings, several keys to cities, some brightly-colored hard candies that Jack admired, and the like.

Jack offered to stash the Wogglebug's flashy necktie in the crate with our other belongings, but the Wogglebug knotted the tie around his slender neck. "I prefer to keep my hard-won love close to my heart," said he.

When the Tin Woodman returned, all seemed ready. Following the others, I trundled on my stiff sofa legs out into the hallway and to the foot of the staircase to the third floor.

"Only nine flights of stairs," said the Scarecrow.

The Wogglebug chuckled. "Take flights to take flight."

"What are you talking about?" Jack Pumpkinhead asked.

"A little joke, my pumpkin-headed friend," said the Wogglebug. "You see, we must walk up these stair flights in order to make a Gump flight. The ascent to the ascent."

The Sawhorse rolled his knot eyes. "He's doing it again."

The Tin Woodman frowned at the Wogglebug. "That's enough of that."

They untied the clothesline that held me together. The Wogglebug leaned my head against the wall. The Scarecrow laid my coiled clothesline beside it, and the Tin Woodman stacked the palm fronds that served as my wings. Jack Pumpkinhead carefully set my broom tail into one corner, then helped the others hoist one of my sofas onto the Sawhorse's back. The sturdy wooden beast started up the stairs with its burden, leaving my other sofa for a second trip. The Scarecrow and the Tin Woodman braced the first sofa's sides, calling out contradictory directions, and the Wogglebug pushed from behind. Jack carried the crate of souvenirs.

I whiled away the minutes till their return with thoughts of the lush forests and fields of the Land of Oz I'd soon see once more. But before the others returned from the roof, two men wearing derby hats descended the stairs.

At the sight of my various pieces waiting in the hallway, they halted in astonishment. One had a black mustache and appeared to be bald under his derby. "What's all this trash doing here?" he asked.

The shorter, rounder one wearing spectacles replied, "Crowds to wade through outside and junk to wade through inside. This hotel purely ain't the quality establishment we were led to believe."

"Downright shoddy," said the first. "We'll check the train schedules and depart."

"Chicago's a mighty disappointment, I must—" The short one with spectacles stopped speaking. He stared at my head leaning against the wall. "Why, Jefferson, look at this trophy head."

"Peculiar animal," said Jefferson. "Someone's notion of a joke, do you suppose?"

I suppressed my urge to bite this Jefferson person and remained silent, hoping the men would go away.

"Decent specimen, I'd call it," said the other. A warm feeling of kinship rose within me. "I'll have it shipped home and tell Ethel I shot it in Alaska. Put an end to her endless complaints about our shooting trips."

My feeling of kinship gave way to alarm. Silently, desperately, I commanded them to leave.

Jefferson laughed. "A good joke—passing it off as proof that you can hit what you aim at. But what will you claim it is?"

"Oh, a rare sort of mountain moose," said the other, lifting the plaque on which my head was mounted. This had gone far enough. "Or a species of reindeer Darwin never—"

"Stop!" I bellowed. "Put me down! Go away!"

They screamed. The short one dropped my head to the floor, chipping my plaque—you can still see the chip. They sprinted down the hallway, limbs flying wildly, clutching at each other to get ahead. They clattered down the stairs to the lobby and were gone, except for a derby one of them had lost. The derby silently bumped down the stairs after them.

My companions from Oz trooped down from the roof.

The Wogglebug picked up my head. "What are you doing lying in the middle of the hall?" he asked.

"Two men tried to walk off with me," I said. "Hurry, and let's go home before any greater mishap occurs."

"Jack," said the Tin Woodman, "stay here to guard the Gump's remaining parts while we carry the second sofa to the roof."

The Wogglebug leaned my head against the wall again. They loaded the remaining sofa onto the Sawhorse and climbed the stairs, leaving Jack Pumpkinhead with me.

As we waited, the hotel's head of housekeeping bustled along the hallway. She approached, running her white-gloved finger along the wainscoting, examining it every few moments, and frowning. When she spotted Jack, she inhaled sharply. "Sir," she said, "are you a guest at this hotel?"

"I was," said Jack. "It's a nice hotel. But it's time to go home. The crowd outside, you see."

The housekeeper pursed her lips. "Very troublesome, indeed, sir," said she. "Bad for business. The manager has repeatedly asked the police to disperse them, but it's no use. I'm very sorry, sir."

"I think," said Jack, "when we go, they'll go."

"Ah," said the housekeeper. "You're with the party from Oz." She smirked humorlessly, then studied my head leaning against the wall, my palm-leaf wings piled on the floor, my coiled clothesline, and my broom tail. "Sir, do these objects belong to you?" she asked Jack, her tone dripping disapproval.

"That's the Gump," said Jack. "The others are taking the rest of him to the roof, while I watch here."

The housekeeper frowned in puzzlement. "So untidy," she murmured.

I spoke up. "Ma'am," I said, "in twenty minutes, we'll have these things cleared from the hallway and you'll never know we were here."

Her shoulders jumped in surprise. "Oh, uh, very good." She reached for my broom tail standing in a corner. "At least I can take this out of your way."

"No, no!" said Jack. "That's the Gump's tail."

"Nonsense," said the housekeeper. "I know hotel property when I see it. I'd recognize this broom anywhere. I shall return it to housekeeping."

"Stop!" I yelled, but she paid no attention. She whipped a white glove off her hand and clutched my tail. Muttering darkly about petty theft of hotel property by guests, she strode back down the hallway to the rear stairs used by hotel employees.

I didn't want to lose my tail. It wasn't much to look at, but it helped in steering when I flew. I concentrated on making the broom wriggle from her grasp. But I've never had much luck in getting my parts to work when they're not joined together.

"Go after her, Jack," I said. "Get my tail back."

Jack hurried off. He's never impressed me as the brightest pumpkin in the patch, so all my nerves trembled as I waited for his return.

Footsteps descended the nearby stairs. The Scarecrow, the Tin Woodman, the Wogglebug, and the Sawhorse appeared again.

"I'm in desperate straits," I said. "The hotel housekeeper took my tail. Jack went after her, but hasn't returned."

The rough fabric on which the Scarecrow's face was painted wrinkled with concern. "We won't fly away from here while any portion of the Gump is missing," he said.

"To do so would be heartless," said the Tin Woodman.

"The Gump's tail is missing, not his heart," said the Sawhorse.

The Wogglebug chuckled. "I suggest," said he, "that we take the rest of the Gump to the roof right away. Jack will follow us when he recovers the tail."

"Let's go," said the Scarecrow, "before the Gump loses anything else."

So they carried my head, my clothesline, and my palm fronds up the nine flights, bumping my nose into walls and doors only a dozen times. On the hotel's broad, flat roof, they tied my sofas together with the clothesline, binding my head to one end and my palm leaf wings to the sofa backs. The day was unseasonably warm, the cloudless blue sky and light breeze perfect for flying.

As the Tin Woodman tied the final knot, the Scarecrow asked, "What's delaying Jack?"

Down in the hotel, Jack hadn't yet recovered my tail. The housekeeper had gone out to sweep the front step of the hotel, but she seemed more intent on threatening the crowd than in sweeping. I guess she was unhappy with the unruly people besieging the hotel. She waved the broom above her head, screeching, and shook dust at them. When they shouted and shook their fists at her in return, she smacked them with the broom.

Inside the hotel lobby, Jack crouched behind a high-backed bench and watched through the glass front doors. He knew the rest of us were waiting. Could he dart out, snatch the broom from the housekeeper, and dart back inside before anyone could catch him? His long wooden legs could run faster than human legs—provided his joints didn't wear out. He had to take the risk.

Jack pushed open a glass door. The crowd clamored for him to grant their wishes. Jack hesitated in the doorway, but he needed to get my tail at any cost.

"Sorry, ma'am," he said, and tore the broom from the housekeeper's grip. Before he could back through the doorway again, dozens of hands caught his wrists, his legs, his clothing, and pulled him into the crowd. Threatening figures loomed all around, shouting demands for magic.

The crowd's roar reached the roof.

"What's happening down there?" asked the Sawhorse.

"I hope it doesn't have anything to do with Jack Pumpkinhead," said the Scarecrow, his painted eyes filling with concern. "But I fear my hope's in vain."

We followed the Scarecrow to the low wall at the edge of the roof. In the street ten stories below, the crowd was tossing around an orange sphere like a big basketball.

The Wogglebug gasped. "The Pumpkinhead's pumpkin head!"

"There's his body!" cried the Tin Woodman, pointing to the mannequin-like frame, arms and legs flying, buffeted about by the crowd. "Poor Jack," he moaned.

One of Jack's hands gripped a broom, trying to hold it safely above the crowd's reach. Joy leaped within me. "My tail!" I boomed. "He's got my tail!"

A cry rang out from the crowd below. "Look! On the roof! They're escaping!"

The streetful of faces turned toward us. A howl of mingled triumph and rage rumbled forth. Like a river, the crowd streamed toward the hotel, whirling into eddies at the entrance and flowing from view into the building.

"They're leaving Jack ruined in the street," said the Tin Woodman. He sounded ready to cry.

"That's nothing to what they'll do to us on the roof," said the Wogglebug.

The Sawhorse snorted. "All those stairs between us and them will discourage those weakly-made meat people."

"They'll be here before you know it," said the Scarecrow. "Remember the elevator."

"When I was caught among them," said the Wogglebug, "their ferocity shocked me."

My palm leaf wings shivered. "I want to go home," I said.

"Can you fly without your tail?" asked the Scarecrow.

"I can go up and down and straight ahead," I said. "Just don't ask me to turn."

"Good enough," said the Scarecrow. "We'll fly up from the roof, then down to pick up Jack—"

"Don't forget my tail," I said.

"—and your tail," said the Scarecrow, "and then take off to find a deserted spot where we'll land and attach your tail again."

"Then home to the Land of Oz?" I asked.

"Then home," said the Scarecrow, nodding.

"Everyone into the Gump!" said the Tin Woodman.

The Scarecrow swung the crate of our bits and mementos onto my sofa seat and flopped in after it. The Wogglebug and the Tin Woodman boosted the Sawhorse, who couldn't get in by himself, and dove in.

"All set?" I asked as I pointed myself toward the front of the hotel. "Off we go!"

The door to the roof banged open. People staggered toward us, panting, scattering beads of perspiration, and screaming, "Magic! We want magic! Grant our wishes!"

"Fly! Fly!" squeaked the Wogglebug.

I flapped my wings and rose as dozens of hands caught my sofa legs and clutched my clothesline. I beat my wings wildly, but the crowd's weight dragged me back down to the roof.

The Scarecrow stood on my seat, cradling the crate of souvenirs. "Let's give them wishes," he said. He pulled out some of the crate's contents and strewed it over the crowd. "Here you go!" he shouted. "Wish all you want on these!"

People grabbed for little falling replicas of the Brooklyn Bridge, the Masonic Temple Building, the Washington Monument, and other sights we'd seen. The Tin Woodman and the Wogglebug reached into the crate and scattered matchboxes, cigarette cards, cartes de visite, and suchlike ephemera.

"Take these for wishes!" called the Wogglebug.

"Wish away!" shouted the Tin Woodman.

The breeze from my wings blew bits and pieces across the grasping crowd. The scrapbook of newspaper clippings beaned one poor woman on the nose.

The Scarecrow shook out the last of the crate's contents and dropped it over the side. The crate splintered on a big man's head. I felt the final greedy hand let go of me to clutch for a magic wish. I shot straight up into the air.

The Wogglebug sighed. "What a relief."

"I wonder how long before they realize we fooled them," said the Tin Woodman.

"We've had exciting experiences in the USA," said the Scarecrow. "But this might top them all."

"Don't forget Jack," said the Sawhorse.

"And my tail," I said. I flew beyond the hotel roof and glided down toward the street. Among bits of trash discarded by the crowd lay Jack's wooden body. One stick-like hand still clutched my broom tail. Jack's other arm waved feebly, as if beckoning. Nearby lay his pumpkin head. Several cracks split its surface.

"Let's be quick," said the Scarecrow. "There weren't enough wishes for the whole crowd. They'll be back to demand more."

"And if they realize those weren't really wishes...." The Tin Woodman trailed off.

As soon as my sofa legs hit the pavement, the Wogglebug and the Tin Woodman hopped out. They lifted Jack's body and helped him climb in. The Scarecrow picked up the pumpkin and gently set it into one corner of the seat. The longest crack ran through one eye and divided the mouth in two.

"I'm afraid Jack's head will never be the same again," said the Scarecrow as he tumbled in.

"Mmh-fff-urg," said Jack's head.

The Wogglebug, holding the broom, leaned out my back end. "No one's spotted us," he said. "I'll tie the broom on."

The hotel doors burst open. People flooded out, yelling. They headed straight for us.

"Fly, Gump!" shouted the Sawhorse.

"Just a moment," said the Wogglebug. "I've nearly got it."

I felt the Wogglebug tying my tail on. It felt so good.

"No time!" shouted the Scarecrow.

I wanted to wait for the final knot, but I flapped my wings and sailed upward.

A man jumped and caught the rear of one sofa, just beside the Wogglebug. I flopped my wings, jostling side to side, trying to dislodge the man. He slipped but caught the Wogglebug's neck with one hand. The Tin Woodman and the Scarecrow grabbed the Wogglebug's legs to stop him from sliding out.

I jounced in the air to shake the man off. His fingers snagged one end of the Wogglebug's necktie, and it whipped from the bug's neck. The man plunged back into the crowd, the necktie clutched in his hand.

The Sawhorse rattled a wooden leg against my antlers. "Go! Go!" he shouted.

I shot up into the sky.

The Wogglebug emitted a piercing cry of despair. "My love! Lost! Lost!" He sank to the sofa seat, clutching his head in all four hands. He mumbled something that I couldn't hear distinctly.

"What did the Wogglebug say?" I asked.

The Tin Woodman shook his head. "It's unfit to repeat in polite company," said he.

We didn't dare return for the necktie. My tail was securely attached, thanks to the Wogglebug, so I soared for home at last. Ah, home! I was never happier to spot the dome of the Emerald City palace glowing on the horizon. Ozma gave us a royal welcome and listened with great interest to all our adventures in the USA.

Jack's head was no good anymore. So he carved himself a new one—badly—since he couldn't see what he was doing. But it served him long enough to carve a better head before that one spoiled. Then he got the idea to grow his own pumpkins, so that he'd never lack for a supply of new heads. Jack's doing fine now.

As for me, I'd finished with traveling, so I had them take me apart again. I've hung here in this back hallway of Ozma's palace ever since. No more gallivanting across the landscape for me. And I'm perfectly content with that.

JINJUR
J.R. Dawson

General Jinjur enjoyed the ending to her story. She did *not* enjoy what people said about the ending.

She had been bothered and badgered by so many paper people and porcelain women about becoming a speaker for their cause, to talk about how she had put down her sword and thirst for conquest and transformed into a nice housewife.

The women in the Emerald City, very queer and very opinionated, believed she had let them down. Once an icon, now she had been brainwashed into living with a *man* when she could be ruling Oz with her army.

Jinjur was no longer a general, and people had feelings about this.

The Munchkin farmer she had married was named Rol. Rolofus, for long. And Rol made her very big world seem so intimate, so safe. There was glory in small things, not just coups and wars and witches. And she deserved nice things, like a flower garden and cooking hot soup on cold nights. She wanted to be in love, and she was in love, so she married.

If nothing else, it showed how powerfully she felt about her husband, that she would give up a revolution for him. Ozma was back, that's what everyone wanted. The Scarecrow was gone, Jinjur had done her part, so let the rest of the world burn the way they'd wanted her to burn.

And she would have her life full of flowers and early morning tea and toast with a Munchkin who said her eyes sparked with the fire of the hottest star in the sky.

It is said that even Princess Ozma didn't mind herself about Jinjur. When her delegates said, "What if Jinjur returns? What if she begins another war?" Ozma would shake her head knowingly and reply in that soft voice, "Oh no, she has given up, she married."

Or at least, this is what Jinjur heard. And it made her like the Princess a little less.

Ozma knew what love was. She clearly loved Dorothy, the little farm girl who followed her around, or maybe Ozma followed the farm girl around … but they were always at each other's side. And what if Dorothy Gale had asked Ozma to give up the world for her? Ozma just might have.

Giving up did not mean losing. What other people called 'giving up,' Jinjur called 'choosing.'

It had actually come as a relief to Jinjur when Ozma defeated her. Jinjur had been Queen for only a little while, and she had hated it. People were needy, opinionated, and there was quite a lot of thinking that went into ruling them. She much rather preferred being angry at her cow on the farm over being yelled at by everyone in the city and beyond.

Rol didn't ever yell. And he forgave her when she yelled. Although she was no longer a general or a queen, she was still Jinjur, and that meant a rage that couldn't be doused sat in her chest.

"I enjoy your fire," Rol said pleasantly. "It's warm in the winter and exciting in the summer."

To love was to find one person who knew you for all your best and worst traits and still sat down to dinner with you.

And Jinjur would have spent the rest of her life sitting in Rol's house, cooking their favorite foods and reading their favorite books and singing their favorite songs, if Rol had not angered a witch.

The more we love something, the more it hurts when it is taken from us.

The witch was not one of the cardinal direction witches, and she wasn't a very powerful witch, but she was powerful enough to turn Rol into a mirror and smash him in front of Jinjur.

But Jinjur had never been the crying type, so she collected the pieces in a blanket while the witch ran away, tied the ends of the blanket together on the end of her large hat pin sword, and started for the Emerald City.

She wasn't silly enough to think that her husband, now broken shards of jagged glass, could understand her. But she spoke to him all the same. Down the yellow brick road, past billboards for Wogglebug's Brain Growth Elixir, and she said, "You know, a really big shoe would do the trick," and laughed to herself.

No one laughed with her.

One time, she had threatened to make him into a stew or a goulash. Back when she had such power and could have done such a thing.

There was a bandit on the road at some point, and they did not recognize Jinjur. They were surprised when Jinjur, full of fury and out of patience, stabbed them full of holes with her hat pin sword.

General Jinjur may have retired, but she still had her sword and her muscle and her memory.

Once, when Dorothy and Ozma came to visit her little house, they looked at her with pity. As if because she was married, she had suddenly lost all her teeth. "Oh, poor Jinjur," Ozma had tutted when they didn't think Jinjur could hear them. Dorothy agreed.

"Spending your life milking cows is such a difficult life. Oh, poor Jinjur."

Those words, 'poor Jinjur,' stuck in Jinjur's teeth like spinach the whole evening, even after they'd gone, and she did not allow herself to cry once she and Rol had gone to bed. But Rol could tell, even without tears, that she was sad. And he scooped her up in his arms, a whole retired General and deposed Queen in his grasp, and he said, "Don't mind their words. They don't know what they don't know."

Her love had never been poor.

And now? Well, Rol was gone. Wives can be brutal, deadly, and Oz help them if they didn't bring her husband back.

She did not have the magic of Glinda. She did not have the birthright of Ozma. She did not have the luck of Dorothy. But she had made her own magic with a sword and a loud voice and rhetoric and the ability to lead a crowd of a thousand women to dethrone a scarecrow king.

The first time she'd met Ozma, Ozma had been under the spell that trapped her in a boy's body. Even still, Jinjur knew Ozma was different, one of her own. She had told Ozma all about the army she was putting together to overthrow Scarecrow, even when she didn't know her and shouldn't have trusted her.

And now she arrived at the Emerald City with the same feeling in her heart, that although Ozma was a silly little girl that Jinjur should not turn to, she was someone who could help.

Jinjur made it to the Emerald City and looked at the Love Magnet, set above the entrance to the town. When had Ozma put it up there? *Why* had she put it up there? Was she really just as conniving as the rest of the rulers before her?

Jinjur decided to go another way into the Emerald City, away from the Love Magnet, so she could see things more clearly. So she snuck in through a trash receptacle.

When she'd left the Emerald City, nothing was green but the glasses people looked through. Now everything was actually painted green. There was a calm here she had not felt before.

No one is perfect, Rol would have said.

But Rol couldn't say anything, because he was several shards of glass in her satchel.

"Pardon me," a man with shaggy clothes and a shaggy beard apologized as he bumped into Jinjur. Jinjur held her parcel closer to her.

"Watch where you walk!" Jinjur snapped. And the man tipped his shaggy hat.

"Apologies," he said. "I will. Oh, and welcome to the Emerald City. I've not seen you before."

Jinjur eyed him. "Can you tell me about why Princess Ozma has the Love Magnet above the entrance?"

The shaggy man looked to the entrance behind them, and then back to Jinjur. "Well," he said, "I think she wants everyone to feel safe and wanted here."

"Or she wants to trick people into loving her," Jinjur said, disappointed.

The shaggy man shrugged. "Maybe she is just a young girl doing her best. See, I gave her the Love Magnet. I used it for many years to keep people from hurting me. Now I'm trying to learn how to trust folks without its magic."

"Because she wants to use it for herself."

"It must be a hard thing, being a ruler," he said.

"I know," Jinjur said.

"But then, it's a hard thing being anyone." The Shaggy Man shrugged again. "I hope, while you're here, you can try to trust as well. Perhaps even make a friend!"

And the shaggy man was gone, whistling down the street.

What a queer fellow.

But something about him reminded her of Rol. Rol, standing in the garden, a black eye from the angry cow he had been milking. But he hadn't been mad at the cow. He'd nursed his face with a towel packed full of ice as he'd said to Jinjur, "It's not her fault. She's got no other way of telling me I am a bad milker."

"She hurt you," Jinjur had protested, on the verge of selling the cow.

"Because I hurt her," Rol had said. "So I'll do better, and she'll do better. We both mean well."

But that was before Rol was glass. Jinjur now went to the palace. She stepped through the protocols of all the guards and the doors, everyone looking at her nervously. A lot of these people,she had fought in the great takeover with her army. Their guns had not been loaded and they hadn't wanted to hurt her army of girls. But the girls had stabbed them, poked and prodded them, taken over the palace. And now the General had returned, for what, these men did not know. To hurt them again? To try and dethrone Ozma? Jinjur wasn't dressed in her regalia. Just her farmgirl pants and blouse and muddy boots, with the parcel on her sword over her shoulder.

Finally, after much rigamarole, she arrived in Ozma's greeting chambers.

Ozma had blossomed like the flowers she wore in her hair. Beautiful, half-fae and all-leader, she looked down at Jinjur from her emerald throne. Her face was blank, with a twinge of nervousness in one eye that she was trying very hard to conceal.

"Jinjur," Ozma said, her ethereal voice singing out through the chambers. "Why have you come before me?"

Jinjur immediately knelt, gently placing the parcel in front of her. "I have a favor to ask," she began. "My husband, Rol, has been transformed by a minor witch and shattered into many pieces. Could you please help me?"

"Of course," Ozma said. "I know how much you love Rol. And the more you love Rol, the less likely you are to try to take my throne."

"I don't care about your throne!" Jinjur snapped. "Honestly, there shouldn't *be* a throne." And then she shut her mouth quickly. Because her rage was getting the best of her. And it could mean Rol would never return.

But Ozma just pleasantly smiled. "How is the farm?"

"It will be better once Rol is returned to it." Jinjur gritted her teeth.

"What made you know you wished to marry and grow up?" Ozma asked.

Jinjur raised her head and looked at the little ruler, realizing Ozma truly wanted to know.

"I fell in love," Jinjur said.

"That's all it was?"

"Yes."

"And to love someone is enough to want to grow up?" Ozma asked. "Well, in that case, I shall probably grow up very soon. I thought it must be more complicated than that."

"You love the farm girl," Jinjur said.

Ozma nodded, her pink lips smiling like little rose buds. "She is so full of tenacity, and now she has moved here for good! No more United States. She and her entire family live in the Emerald City."

"The city you enchant with a Love Magnet," Jinjur said pointedly.

Ozma nodded. "Oh, only as a precaution, so we don't see any more wars. Or takeovers," she said. "It is for visitors. Not for residents."

"I don't trust people who are good at ruling," Jinjur said.

"You once ruled," she said.

"And I was not a good ruler," Jinjur said. "I was very relieved when you usurped me."

Ozma looked perplexed, her brow furrowed in the frame of her perfect curled hair and her perfect flower crown. "So why don't you trust me? You came here to ask me for help, and also to belittle me? You do still have that temper, I suppose."

Jinjur narrowed her eyes. "You keep the Wizard as a court jester. He murdered your father. Why not kill him?"

"What good will that do?" Ozma said. "It will only bring more rage."

"Sometimes, rage is good. Fire is powerful."

"And sometimes, fire burns us and all around us. Sometimes, we need gentleness as well."

And Jinjur thought about Rol, holding her in bed. Petting the cow, singing to her, even with a shiner on his face.

She never thought Rol weak. Just as Rol never thought her evil.

Ozma cocked her head. "I will ask my magic belt to help us."

Jinjur put her sack down on the floor, undid the blanket, and put the mirror shards into a shape like one would complete a puzzle. "There. Right there. Bring him back."

"Could you put your cloth over him to make the spell work best?" Ozma said. "People don't like to change so much when being looked at."

"As long as you don't move him and I can see his form shift." Jinjur put her blanket over the broken pieces. "No funny business."

Ozma put on the jeweled belt over her beautiful dress and stroked it gently as if it was a child. "Please, old friend," she said to the belt, "will you return Rol to Munchkin form?"

"Just the way he was," Jinjur added. You could never be too careful with magic.

"Just the way he was," Ozma repeated, and then looked to the cloth on the floor. "It should only be a moment."

The thing under the cloth grew, stood, was now less mirror-shaped and more person-shaped. It was very quick, as most magic was here in Oz. A shattered life, pieced back together as if it was nothing. But it was everything.

Rol returned to her.

Rol, her Rol, scooped her up in his arms. She then let herself cry, in front of Ozma. Rol dried her tears.

"I am never letting go of you ever again," she sobbed.

Rol smiled, only a small cut on his chin now, as if a glass shard was out of place. "My dear, even as a bag full of broken mirror, I'm yours."

"Oh, Rol!" Jinjur held him closer. "While that might be true, I'd much rather you be able to speak and hold me. Broken mirrors can't milk the cow."

Rol laughed. "Yes, that's why you missed me."

Ozma stepped closer off her dais. "He is returned to you, the man for whom you gave up a kingdom."

And both of the farmers looked to the princess.

"Rol and Jinjur," Ozma bowed to them, "please have a lovely rest of your day here. And know you are always welcome in the Emerald City, as long as you don't cause any trouble."

Jinjur gave a little smile. "I can't make such a big promise. But I thank you for giving me back my life."

Ozma also smiled, and opened her arms. "May it be long and full of love."

There was something in the way the princess smiled, or perhaps in the way she spoke to Jinjur, that made Jinjur want to trust her.

"I will send you a thank you letter when I return home," Jinjur offered.

Ozma's grin widened. "Thank you, friend."

Friend.

And so, Jinjur and Rol left behind the Emerald City she'd once conquered. Hand in hand, they followed the yellow brick road back to their angry cow, their snug bed, and the small glory of home.

THE FIELD MOUSE QUEEN TAKES FLIGHT
Jendia Gammon

The Queen of the Field Mice of Oz was known for her storied rule and leadership, and also for rescuing Princess Dorothy, Toto, and the Cowardly Lion from the deadly poppies that swayed their sinister, scarlet heads above the burrows of her domain. What she was *not* known for was taking a vacation.

For starters, she had many children; countless, it may be believed, who skittered and clambered and scurried and sniffed and did all the things mice will do, while being under both their mouse queen's protection, and that of Ozma, ruler of Oz. Ozma was a great friend of the Field Mouse Queen, who had, like Ozma, gone by other names over the course of her whiskered life. Being a wise fairy, Ozma had ensured the small, silver-grey-brown mouse would continue her rule over her extensive domain without interfering with the general governance of Oz. Ozma also, it may be said confidently, knew when her subjects needed something but might never get around to asking for it. So it was that she sent a message by dragonfly to another friend one late, late summer day, when the long grasses of the rolling meadows outside the great City began to burnish and bend, and the air smelled of honey and apples and bread and sweet blue flowers of all sorts…as well as dizzying poppies.

The mice, however, were so small that the poppies never affected them. In fact, the Field Mouse Queen had advocated they should remain, rather than be cut, for those flowers served other purposes for the pollinators and detritivores that either bounced gently above them or worked with decaying matter underground. And also, in late summer, many of them began to go to seed. A fine feast for any royal court, but especially for any mouse; the gentle roasting of poppy seeds by tiny mouse hands twitching their tails in excitement heralded the beginning of harvest season, and then autumn. So the harvest was a bustling time of lavish balls, with mouse and rat and vole and shrew and both larger and smaller guests of field and forest cavorting under the Harvest Moon. The

Queen of the Field Mice loved that time of year, but she had begun to admit, after many wheelings of sun and stars overhead, that sometimes, she would have liked to have allowed some of her more mature children to take the lead for a change, to sit out the society season.

She, as Queen of all mice in the Land of Oz, must choose the Acorn out of a parade of young mice from all corners of Oz, and its countries: Winkie, Gillikin, Munchkin, Quadling, and of course the Emerald City itself. This was the highest mouse society honor: the Acorn of the Harvest Season. For that season, it was the only opportunity for a mouse from any lineage to wear a crown bestowed by the Queen: that of a bronze acorn, studded with the tiniest, finest topaz crystals, gifted long ago by a Winkie miner. And while the larger denizens of the Land of Oz might never realize it in their daily lives that time of year, every little hillock and hollow and tiny trail rustled and rippled with a great many mice streaming in for the crowning of their society at that harvest ball.

It amused the Queen to do this, as, in her younger days, she had enjoyed parties and balls as a little mouse princess. She also adored the harvest feast with snippets of fresh apple; slivers of nutty, hard cheeses (kindly donated from a Munchkin farmer); droplets of honeydew and hyssop syrup and maple sap in wee goblets; freshets of mineral water; poppy mead and perry and blackberry wine, and so on. It was also a spectacle to behold, the dancing of many twinkling whiskers, the chatters and whispers and laughter and general gaiety, the frilly outfits, the occasional fancy masks, the decorative bows and diadems on the tails of the mice. Oh! She did love it.

But *this* year. *This* year, she sighed.

Far away to the South, in Quadling Country, Glinda smirked to herself and tossed back her deep red curls as she stood from where she had been sitting. Just behind her, a dragonfly landed on a bouquet of fresh flowers. Before her lay open the great book that she used to keep up with all things and all times. And upon its pages, the letters bled forth: *The Queen of the Field Mice sighed.* Glinda leaned back and steepled her long, ruby-tipped fingers under her chin and nodded to herself. The dragonfly then flew to her shoulder and whispered something to her that only its own kind and Glinda might understand. Then the gauzy-winged insect flew off, shimmering, and Glinda watched it go.

"It is time to have a bit of a chat with an old friend," she murmured, brushing her glistening skirts, spun from threads made of garnet, ruby, tourmaline, and rose quartz. She clapped her hands lightly, and soon a maiden in a smart pink outfit appeared. That young woman bowed to the

Witch of the South. "Come closer, child," bade Glinda, "for I have a special message." The young woman bent forward, and Glinda whispered in her ear. Then the girl's eyebrows lifted, but she bowed, smiling, and turned. Glinda nodded to herself, lost in happy thoughts for several minutes, before turning back to her great book, where letters seeped into its pages faster than lightning, faster than fleeting memories. She wanted to learn what might happen next...

Dawn broke upon the fields that stretched between the gleaming spires of the Emerald City, over into Munchkin country, where the fences were painted every hue of blue to match the blue flowers of that land, and its bluegrass shivered and sparkled with morning dew. Closer to the city, the fields were rich green, and the fences also. There were delicate lime-hued and teal green flowers bobbing there. It made the poppies, which were now either dropping their petals or nearly so, stand out all the more.

The Queen of the Field Mice had awakened after a fitful night of dreaming about harvest preparations. She'd even dreamed that the Acorn Crown had been made of brown sugar that crumbled upon its chosen wearer. That made her snort in her dream, or so she thought.

But no, it was another snort that woke her.

She blinked, fully awake now, whiskers twitching, her dark eyes gleaming like little beads of onyx. She sometimes liked to sleep in a little hollow, on a bed filled with dandelion seed tufts, rather than in the warrens beneath her. Her excuse was that she wanted to remain vigilant at all times for her mouse dominion, but deep in her heart, she really preferred being outside so that she could see the stars at night, and then watch the sunrise send its long, golden shafts of light over the wakening fields. She began to groom herself as she listened for the sound she'd heard. She had just cleaned her silvery-grey fur and brushed off her long tail when she heard it again.

Snort-honk! Snort-honk!

She squinted up at a great tree at the edge of the boundary between Munchkin Country and the Emerald City. At its top there was a snag, and within that sat a broad, massive bowl made of sticks, grasses, tufts of moss, and all manner of other items. It was a nest, an eagle's nest, to be precise. And two eagles were working on it just then! They sorted and adjusted several sticks, and fussed and kissed their beaks as they did so.

"Ah," the Queen of the Field Mice said to herself, "they are preparing for a new season this winter! I wonder how many eggs there might be."

Snort-honk! Snort-honk!

There came a great flapping of wings, and an immense eagle burst from the top of the nest. It was then followed by another.

Some deep, ancient mammalian instinct sent her running for cover, although these days, she knew that she truly had nothing to fear under Ozma's protective rule. The Land of Oz provided for all who lived there in its own ways, with great fairy magic. But still. Casting her gaze left and right, the Queen could see that her subjects were also spooked, and had dashed into the undergrowth or beneath the earth altogether. But she was a Queen! And she was *their* queen. She must show them all bravery.

"Fear not!" she called in her high-pitched little mouse voice. "No harm will come to you."

"Of course-SNORT-HONK-not!" bellowed a voice.

Despite herself, the Queen gave a little squeak: for above her a great shadow gave way to one of the two immense eagles. The other circled in the air above. Every bit of fur on the Queen's body stood on end. The eagle was landing! In front of her! And it was *huge*. One quick glance at the flying companion told her this was the lady eagle, and her companion, who was smaller, was the sir.

She drew herself up as tall as she could before this magnificent lady eagle, who stared down her golden beak with piercing silver eyes under a white feather cap. The Queen of the Field Mice needed no scepter or cloak, and not even her crown, for her command was obvious. But for all that, she was still surprised that the eagle *bowed*.

Then she stood in a heraldic pose and threw her great beak skyward. *SNORT-HONK!* Her husband, soaring, responded in his own eagle language.

"What brings you to the lands of the field mice, Madam Eagle? I see a nest in that tall tree yonder." And the Queen's tail twitched as she looked up at the fearsome, sharp beak, and down at the great, golden talons…larger than her own body. She swallowed and fought a shaking tremor in her whiskers. *I may be safe, it is true,* she thought, *but the wilder days of yore remind me of what once was. Will Madam remember as well?*

The lady eagle tossed her proud head toward the tall tree. "We have found this beautiful old snag, and an ancient nest. See its great size! Many eaglets have been born there. But that is not the only reason we are here."

"And what," the Queen of the Field Mice squeaked, "are your…other reasons?"

Another snortle escaped Madam Eagle. "Our crops are full, o Queen, and not of your kith and kin, nor shall they be!"

"Oh, well, that's a relief," the Queen caught herself saying with a nervous laugh. She felt then that time had slipped backward many years, for in Oz no one aged visibly while they lived there. She could just barely remember her days as a young mouse, bounding over grass archways and clambering carefully through thorns to snatch fat berries. Back then, she had not been a queen; she had been a mouse princess newly anointed, and the land had been tangled and wild and at times quite terrifying, far more even than for any mouse outside of Oz. For in those days, there had been monsters aplenty: kalidahs and vicious beasts without names that slinked out of deep crevices in the earth and between fairyland and the outside world. She shuddered. Madam Eagle watched her intently.

It was then that the Queen spied a small scarlet ribbon around the right talon of the great bird.

"You're wearing red, Madam Eagle," she noted.

The bird dipped her massive, elegant head. "You are astute, Your Highness. I hail from Quadling Country."

The Queen's little ears perked up; the rising sun shone through them, setting them aglow like tiny petals. "What might bring you from that fair land?" she asked Madam Eagle.

"I was asked a favor by the witch, Glinda," said Madam Eagle. "I at first protested, for nesting season happens soon. But the Good Witch said, 'One may find a new perspective, unlooked-for.' She is, after all, known for being a bit cryptic," Madam Eagle added with a honk. She glanced up at her mate, who now perched close by on a lower branch in a tall pine. He sent out a high-pitched set of chortles. Madam Eagle squawked back in four shirt bursts, so her husband relaxed and began grooming his feathers from his perch.

"That is Glinda, certainly," agreed the Queen. But she was intrigued. Glinda rarely sent messengers forth, and in fact tended to move of her own accord throughout the Land of Oz. Like the Queen, she was rather independent; they understood each other in that way. It had been a long time since the Queen of the Field Mice had ventured so far South, but now she thought fondly of the vivid reds and pinks and magentas of the flowers and fruits there, and it was warmer as well. Her eyes glazed over for a moment. Shaking her head, she asked, "What favor has Glinda asked, if you don't mind?"

Madam Eagle shook her wings and straightened her proud shoulders.

"I have been asked," she said, impressively stretching out her wings just a bit, "to give you a day off."

The Queen of the Field Mice felt her jaw go slack as she stared up at the huge bird.

"I…what?" she stammered, taken rather by surprise by such a proclamation. "What on clovered earth made her think that?"

Madam Eagle leaned slowly, frighteningly down until her eyes locked onto the mouse queen's.

In a low, whistling voice, she said, "I do not question the ways of the Witch of the South. For we are friends, of a kind, but she is the wisest of us all."

That is true, the Queen managed to think, still holding back a wall of near panic within herself as she faced the eagle.

"I am afraid I do not understand," the Queen murmured, "why an eagle—er, such an extraordinary herald, I should say—ought to be sent to me for such a message."

Madam Eagle stood up again, and the Queen could swear that the lady eagle winked up at her husband, who then launched himself back up to the nest tree.

"I have the keenest sight of any animal in the land by day," Madam Eagle said proudly. "I am tasked with taking you on a journey, to give you the day off. I happily oblige."

Oh, how the Queen of the Field Mice protested then. "I can't possibly! The Acorn Crown! The celebrations! The harvest! The…the…" She was at a loss for squeaks.

A long stream of snort-honk-chuckles erupted from Madam Eagle, and her shoulders shook. "I begin to see now why you need the day off! As a fellow mother, dearest Queen of the Field Mice, we all need a day off. Between nesting, between hunting—er, eating—between feeding the eaglets—er, mouse pups. I mean, not *actually* feeding *them* the—"

Madam Eagle shook her head in deep embarrassment as the Queen shivered on her hind legs, her front paws on her hips, her tail whipping to and fro behind her.

And then she *laughed*. She laughed like she hadn't since she was a pup herself, her eyes fully open and her legs springy as a young mouse. Her high, tinkling laugh echoed over the hills, and all the other mice dared to peek at her, facing the huge eagle, laughing. Slowly, they crept forth to watch in awe, and then in glee, and then pride at their queen. The Queen of the Field Mice laughed at a huge eagle! What better queen, aside from Ozma herself, could they have asked for? they chattered to each other.

The Queen smirked, setting her whiskers trembling. Then she called upon her staff, and they scurried forth, keeping a respectful distance from the enormous former apex predator, Madam Eagle. They, too, held that long buried memory of a different time and place. But if their queen could stand strong, so could they.

"My dear kith and kin," she said to her grown children and her maids, "I have decided to take a vacation."

A ripple of the tiniest gasps and squeals undulated among the grasses and under the poppy seedheads.

"Yes," the Queen continued, "we have much to celebrate. And I see that all the harvest preparations have been made, the Acorn Crown is polished almost to copper, the food is ready, and everything is beautiful." She admired the streamers and little bells and wildflower clusters tied with vivid string, the small, bright tents and tables made of mushrooms. "And I shall rejoin you soon enough. But I am taking a break. I trust that everymouse here will enjoy themselves, and feast upon the fruits of the harvest. It is a full moon tonight as well! May you dance beneath it in joy and pride in another summer that wafts out and away, and we shall let autumn glide in."

She clapped her tiny paws, and then everyone cheered. But she stood, hesitant, staring up at Madam Eagle.

In the tiniest little mouse voice, but one which the eagle could hear easily, she whispered, "I do not know how to take a vacation."

Madam Eagle threw back her head and let out another honk. "Easy," she said to the little Queen. "Climb on my back."

The Queen of the Field Mice swallowed. "In all my days, never once have I even dreamed of climbing upon the back of an eagle," she admitted to the great bird.

"But you *have* dreamed of taking a break," noted Madam Eagle.

"I have," the Queen admitted.

So up she clambered, quick as a wink.

"You are nimbler than the flying squirrels who annoy us in our nests at night," Madam Eagle said.

"I should give them a talking to about doing that!" the Queen tsked.

Now she was at the nape of Madam Eagle's neck, where the white feathers changed to dark russet brown. She looked down at her queendom, and all the mice were waving their handkerchiefs up at her, some laughing, some cheering, some actually weeping.

"I shall return soon!" she called down to them. She felt rather as though she might be headed to the moon.

But nothing prepared her for the ripple of muscle beneath her feet, and she clung carefully to the bird's feathers as Madam Eagle pulsed her powerful wings. *Thawoosh, thawoosh!* The wings carved the air as Madam Eagle soared higher.

"Oh, oh!" cried the Queen of the Field Mice. They were now so high that she could barely see her subjects below. And then, within a minute, they flew high above the trees, above the nest, even…and Sir Eagle chortled at them as they flew away from him.

Over the hills, around the Emerald City, down into valleys they flew, the wind shrieking in the mouse queen's delicate ears, her fur ruffled constantly. But the smells! The smells of fields, forests, rivers, distant rain, breakfasts being cooked by people below; and all the sights of the great Land of Oz itself, in all directions. How vivid they all were! Although she, like everyone in Oz, knew that beyond that horizon lay a vast, impenetrable, horrible desert, where nothing could survive, and beyond that, the fairylands of Ev and Ix and so on. She gazed up, and quite suddenly Madam Eagle carried them through a cloud. There, diaphanous sky fairies waved and laughed, just as amazed by the little mouse queen's presence as she was by theirs.

And then, down, down, down, in a long spiral, Madam Eagle took her over fields of red and pink, south into Quadling Country. The shimmering halls of Glinda lay there, entwined with vivid bougainvillea and columbine and bright red and fuchsia roses. Madam Eagle turned and angled lower, and swept right onto the balcony of the Witch of the South, who stood smiling, waiting to meet them.

With utmost care, Madam Eagle lowered down to allow the Queen of the Field Mice to descend from her back, and she did so in one quick slide. Glinda's helpers arrived to set food and drink at a table carved out of pale pink granite with veins of garnet and silver. For Glinda, there stood a flute of a pink sparkling beverage, with a raspberry in its base. For Madam Eagle, there rested a plate of red-tinged slabs of protein of unknown origin (truthfully, the Queen of the Field Mice did not wish to know its source). And for the little mouse queen herself, there sat a bowl filled to the brim with jewellike raspberries, strawberries, red currants, and a few chunks of sharp white cheese.

"Dear Queen," laughed Glinda, lovely and ethereal as ever, but with a deep, wise mirth to her ageless face, "it has been too long since we have shared a meal. Now, tell me all about the doings of your queendom."

The Queen of the Field Mice began recounting her everyday duties as ruler of all the mice in Oz, of the preparations for the harvest celebrations, and about her many children and their descendants who came from far and near. But Glinda held up her hand.

"Thank you, dear friend," said the elegant red-haired sorceress. "Now, I want to hear about *you*. What stars have you seen at night?"

The mouse queen twitched her whiskers, wondering how Glinda might know about that.

Is she really that *wise?* she wondered.

"Well, dearest Glinda, the shield maid-mouse is high in the sky now, with her sharp reed sword," answered the Queen dreamily, thinking of the night sky. "To the north, the aurora is faint and pink-green like a bud in the sky, unfolding. And to the south, of course, there is the archer mouse, his bow of spider silk pulled back, his splinter arrow ready..."

So they chatted about stars and constellations, and about the comings and goings through the land toward the Emerald City. The Queen of the Field Mice felt a deep, restful pleasure chatting with Glinda, while Madam Eagle preened and listened and sunned herself. They would all be working hard to prepare for winter, even in Oz where it wasn't quite so fierce. But in Glinda's land, summer still lingered both in fruit and field, and in friendship as well. The sun began to slide, and Madam Eagle glanced at Glinda, who winked slyly back at her. The witch would not rush her friend. This was her vacation, after all.

But the Queen of the Field Mice shook herself out of her reverie, and then stood brightly, before bowing to Glinda.

"Ah, but that is my task, dear friend," chided Glinda gently, smiling, and she then bowed to the little queen. "You are a queen, after all!"

"I must return," said the field mouse queen. "It is harvest time, and I must choose the Acorn tonight, as the moon will rise soon." She sighed in pleasure and gazed up at Madam Eagle. "I am ready, friend eagle," she said firmly, in a commanding but fair tone that only a queen might use, regardless of her size.

"I may send for you again," Glinda told her, in the canny tone that only a powerful sorceress such as she might use... or that a true friend might.

The Queen of the Field Mice then sprang upon the back of Madam Eagle.

"Until the next vacation, then!" she called to Glinda, who waved to her little friend as Madam Eagle took her high in the sky, headed north.

To the East, the moon began to rise, and Madam Eagle chortled out to the owls that had begun to make their own music.

"An eagle, carrying a mouse!" cried they, in their hoots and howls.

"Two mothers, taking a break," called Madam Eagle back to them.

And no animal in Oz had anything bad to say about that.

As the last of the twilight melted away, and the glistening Emerald City lit up for the evening in the distance, Madam Eagle carried the Queen of the Field Mice back to her home, where tiny bobbing lights and every imaginable little creature, mammal or bird or nightjar or insect, had come forth to celebrate the harvest. They all gasped as the eagle slowed and coasted down to land. The Queen of the Field Mice slid neatly off Madam Eagle's back, and with a long, meaningful look between the two vastly different creatures, the queen nodded.

"Thank you. I needed that," she said to her feathered new friend, who said "Snort-honk!" and flew to roost with Sir Eagle for the night. Whether or not they might stay for nesting season, the Queen was not sure. Only the eagles knew such things.

As for tonight, that was mouse business. And she was leader of all the mice in the Land of Oz, and tonight, the little queen would do something unprecedented. She would relax and have fun.

In memory of Sandy Steers for her tireless advocacy of the Big Bear eagles and their habitat, and in honor of Jackie and Shadow and their eaglets.

THE EMERALD HEART
Helen Glynn Jones

"What are we supposed to do with this?"

"Dunno. She's a bit less lively than the other one."

"Magic, though, ain't she? Has to be, because of *her* what left her here? Plus you can *feel* it."

Belingor said nothing, though he rustled his branches in a way that made the leaves fall from them, pattering to the forest floor like rain. The baby, cradled in the crook of one of his gnarled branches, whimpered, wrinkling her perfect button nose, blinking eyes that were already turning from deep blue to green.

"Perhaps we should tell her a story or somethin," another of the trees said, leaning in with a sound of creaking timber. "Children like that, don't they? Just until *she* comes back."

"We could tell her about the other one. The one who woke us. Feels like somethin' she'd like to know."

"She's a *baby*. How d'you know what she'd like to know?"

Belingor harrumphed, the noise drowning out the chatter of everyone else. They waited, then. Because he was the first one made, and so best settled to tell the tale.

A small hand, like a star against the dark wood, waved free of the soft blanket wrapped around the baby's tiny form. She stared up at him and laughed, a sound like a bubbling stream, like the other one who'd come to them, long ago, and wrought her magic on them all. Belingor cleared his throat, and the baby giggled again.

"It's like this, see."

The forest hushed, as Belingor began to tell their tale…

She ran through the forest, light on her slipper-clad feet, like a leaf riding a summer zephyr. Her gauzy dress snagged on twigs, leaving little flutters of fabric like cobwebs, her hair the red-gold of an autumn leaf catching flickers of light.

She was laughing, at first. As though it was a game. Perhaps it started that way. Perhaps she didn't realize that what stalked her had darkness at its heart.

The Kalidah that hunted her was young, the tiger-striped fur on its head still fluffy, the deep brown bear body still chunky and ungainly, like a misshapen child's toy. Perhaps that's what she thought it was when she first came across it.

Though the power the forest sensed in her ran so very deep, it seemed somehow wrong to think she wouldn't have at least had some inkling.

The trees sighed and rustled, pathways opening before her, closing behind her, as the forest did what it could to help. Distress signals darted along branches, fizzed through root systems, clearing the way ahead of her as she ran, like a pale ghost among the deep green.

But there was only so much they could do. Soon she would reach the end of the woods and of their protection, such as it was. More Kalidah waited in the open fields beyond, tiger-striped and bear-clawed, death walking on two legs, as it so often did. Worry and anger and sorrow and regret rustled through the forest as the girl neared the row of trees that held their borders, a barrier between the woodland world and all that lay outside.

They would not look away, though, when the Kalidah took her. For it was inevitable, one way or another. The creature was closing in on her, moving swiftly, claws extended in anticipation of the kill. Others moved in the meadow, alerted by the sound of her passage. It wouldn't be easy to watch, but the forest wouldn't let her die alone.

She gained the edge of the trees. The creature reached for her.

The forest held its breath.

But she did not die.

Oz was a magical place; the trees all knew that. Felt the shimmer of power in the air around them, in the earth that held their roots. In every leaf and branch and twig, ever since Lurline had cast her spells, making Oz into the wondrous place that it was.

That power also extended into its inhabitants. And this girl, it seemed, held far more than her fair share. As the Kalidah reached for her, she evaded its swiping claws, pirouetting like a dancer between two trees at the very edge of the woods. She glanced one way, then the other, before dropping to her knees as though in supplication. The Kalidah threw back its head and roared, revealing stained ivory fangs, curving death personified.

The girl simply tilted her head to one side, like a bird. Then she smiled. It was a kind smile, dazzling in its beauty, her blue eyes wide. The Kalidah paused, then mirrored her head tilt, still smiling its razorblade smile. Playing with her, cat and mouse.

Except the Kalidah was the mouse, and did not realize.

The girl plunged her hands into the soil and closed her eyes, still smiling that beatific smile. Vines emerged from the forest floor like whips, ensnaring the Kalidah, wrapping around its torso, its arms and legs, one curling like a snake around its neck. The creature mewled and whimpered, wide-eyed, now the youngling rather than the predator. Those waiting in the meadow roared in response, though none dared to come closer. They knew, now, what a mistake that would be.

The girl opened her eyes. "It's not very nice to chase people, you know." Her voice was like a bell, ringing clear. A line appeared between her brows. "These woods are for everyone to use, not just you."

The Kalidah snarled and lunged at her, but the vines held firm. "You just looked so very tasty," it growled. "And you were all alone."

"I might be alone, but I am not unprotected." Her tone was mild, but there was a thread of something deeper beneath it, a match to the power welling from her hands, still plunged into the soil. "As you can see."

"Don't kill me, please," the Kalidah whined, sagging against the vines, tears rolling from its green eyes. The forest rustled in warning. A ploy, rather than true contrition. The creature was still dangerous, and perhaps one fewer in the world would be a better thing than not.

"I'm not going to kill you," the girl said, her tone calm as the surface of a forest pond, the depths hidden. "Your death is not for me to decide. Just as mine is not yours."

"But… then…"

"You can stay here for a while," she said. "I don't expect you to think about what you've done, for all you've done is be true to who you are. To *what* you are. I cannot be angry about that. This is a lesson, that's all. That not every creature you hunt is defenseless."

The Kalidah moaned. The forest sighed. Such mercy, such grace! Truly, this girl was someone extraordinary. As though she heard their approval, the girl looked up and smiled.

"As for you, my dearest trees, you have protected me, and for that I am grateful. This is a special place to me, for so many reasons. Would you like to continue protecting not just me, but all those who live in the woods?"

The forest swayed and hummed its approval, joy coursing through every twisting pathway, shaking leaves and branches.

The girl's smile deepened. "Then here are two gifts from me, as thanks for all that you do. The first is my name, for it is Glinda. The second is this."

She closed her eyes again, her head going back slightly. Power surged, glittering like fireflies, coursing through earth into root and trunk, into branch and twig.

And the trees came to life.

All along the border of the woods, roots stretched further down, anchoring into deep bedrock, holding tight. Bark split and peeled, new wood the color of straw bursting through as branches lengthened and thickened at the base, transforming into flexible reaching limbs with twigs that curled like fingers, flexing against the canopy of leaves. Timber groaned, trunks twisting then reshaping themselves, great maws opening as the trees roared their awakening, as their eyes opened, their ears cleared, the sounds and sights of the forest magnified. Leaves fell like rain, the earth and air shuddering as the entire outer edge of the forest was transformed into a chain of strength and fury with one purpose.

To protect.

And all the while, a girl knelt, her hands buried deep in the loamy earth, her eyes closed, her skirts settling around her like the petals of a flower, lovely as spring, deadly as winter.

The Kalidah, finally realizing the magnitude of its error, roared and howled, foaming at the mouth, as the two trees closest to the creature reached out with their branches and dug jagged fingers into its shoulders, holding it in place.

Glinda stood, shaking dark soil from her delicate fingers, barely a ringlet out of place. She gleamed with power, a luminous globe all around her for a moment, as though she was a lantern giving off her own light.

"Be gentle with him," she said, laying a hand on the trees. "He is only a baby, after all."

"How… how long shall we keep him like this?" Belingor, for it was he who first dared to speak, asked the question. And there was wonder in his tone as he found his voice, as he realized his new power.

"A day is long enough, my dear fighting trees," Glinda said. "Maybe even less, if he behaves himself. Or his parents come looking for him."

"So be it." The trees bowed their assent, letting leaves fall softly around Glinda as she slipped back into the woods, a pale glimmer against the greeny dark.

And so it came to pass, when she came into her full power, that Glinda built her palace deep in the woods, studded with rubies and bright as the dawn. It still stands, the forest and her fighting trees still watching, still protecting, still grateful for the gift of magic from a young girl who was so much more than she seemed.

"Like this one. She's also more than she seems," said one of the trees, bending forward to peer at the baby, still tucked in the curve where branch met trunk. Her eyes were closing, lashes brushing her soft downy cheeks as Belingor ended the tale of how they were all made.

"She is."

Another voice, one that made them all still. A voice threaded with thunder, with magic, with the very elements of the earth. The forest waited, breath held, as she continued to speak.

"And so are you, my friends. Faithful guardians of the south, and of those who dwell in my woods. There was no one else I could trust with my most precious gift of all."

She stood at the edge of the trees, her head level with their leafy tops, her hair flowing like her robes, her beauty so dazzling it almost hurt the eye to see.

"My lady Lurline." Belingor bowed as best he was able, keeping the baby safe in the crook of his arm. The other trees also bowed, a rustle of noise like a wave sweeping along the edge of the forest.

"Dear Belingor," she said, reaching one gleaming finger to caress his bark. "Such a wonderful job you've done, all these years." Her finger moved, feather-light, along the curve of the baby's cheek, and her radiance dimmed somewhat, her brilliant gaze turning down. "It's why I knew I could leave her with you. My sweet girl, my princess of Oz. Please, keep her safe until her father comes to get her."

"Her father? How will we know who he is? We don't wanna just give her to anybody."

Lurline smiled, but there was sadness in it, like a cloud crossing the sun. "You'll know him. He is a king, after all. But he is also my love, the one with whom I chose to create this precious life, and one whose life is far shorter than my own. He will keep her safe, though there will be dark times. I cannot always be with you, for there are other worlds that need me. But she needs to be here, for she will be queen of you all, one day."

Belingor looked down at the tiny baby, like a curl of pearl against the roughness of bark and branch, and his heart, such as it was, swelled, sap rising and running to the tips of his twigs. "Does she... My lady, what is her name?"

"Her name is Ozma." Power thrummed in Lurline's voice. "She that was, and always will be. My emerald heart."

THE INN AT THE EDGE OF OZ
Ernie Chiara

At the edge of the desert between Oz and Ev, where sand-strewn trails become dirt-packed roads leading travelers out of the scorching hot sun into a dusty old town where the sun is only slightly less scorching, there sat an Inn called The Wayward Crowns and not much else. And if you listened closely as the wind died down, you could just make out the faint melody from an old tink-plucker carrying on the breeze as if beckoning newcomers to wander on in.

But on a particularly sultry day, as the door to the inn flew open, the folks inside quit chattering, and even the man in the armbands sitting at the old tink-plucker quit plucking its tinks. All went silent. And every head turned to stare at the figures with backlit silhouettes outlined in the glare of the doorway.

A woman gasped. A kitten fled. A child hid their face behind a mother's skirts.

And the shadow of a cloaked man in a harness on the back of a towering figure with wheels for feet and great clockwork hands stretched out onto the old plank floor of The Wayward Crowns. With arms as long as her legs, the figure held in her lithe mechanical grip what looked to be a great brass lantern frame, glassless and empty but for a severed human head. While her other hand reached up behind her, plucked the cloaked man from his harness, and lowered him gently to the floor.

"Greetings," said the man, brushing his cloak aside and shaking the dust from his long, grey beard. "We're nothing to be fearful of. Just a traveler and his companions. This, here, is my friend Alaxis." He gestured towards the figure who'd just set him down. Half again as tall as the tallest patron present, Alaxis bowed deep with a flourish, crossing a great lanky arm and copper hand over her chest and rolling one wheeled leg behind the other.

"Well met, all," spoke the Wheeler, for that is what she was. Or so she was always told, though never once believed it.

"And I bet at least one of you lot are out looking for a little head," said the head in the brass-framed carrier with a smirk, then scanned the crowd for a reaction.

"Now you behave, Nick Chopper," said the man in the cloak as he took the brass carrier from Alaxis's grip.

"Welcome to The Wayward Crowns, and well met, I'm sure." A grey-haired man in a smock and rolled-up sleeves came around the bar to greet them. "I'm JJ, and this is my wife, Sandy." He waved a hand toward the woman behind the bar, who narrowed her eyes and harrumphed. Then, turning toward the old tink-plucker in the corner, JJ shouted, "Joe Tunes, the music if you please."

And with that, the man in the armbands picked up plucking right where he'd left off, and the patrons went back to their drinks and their murmurings.

"I didn't quite catch your name." JJ glanced sideways to the cloaked man as he directed them all toward the bar.

Placing Nick Chopper on the counter and guiding Alaxis to a stool, the man leaned across the bar towards the innkeeper and replied in a low voice, "We've come a long way to meet someone here."

JJ's brows rose, and his eyes darted toward a table in the back of the room before locking back on the man before him. "That didn't answer my question."

The man patted his cloak flat and brushed off the front of his pants, then reached into his pocket for a coin purse which he set on the bar with a clink. "I tell you what, '*JJ*.' You tell me your name, and I'll tell you mine." The corner of his mouth rose ever so slightly. "Or, better yet, if I can guess who you *really* are, you buy my friends a round of drinks. And if I'm wrong, we'll take the drinks anyway, and I'll pay you for them fairly."

JJ blanched. "W-what do you mean by this? I told you, I'm JJ and my wife is—"

"Your wife is Sandy. Yes, so you said." He placed a finger to the side of his round, bald head. "But I know better, Jol Jemkiph Soforth, and I know that you and your wife, So'on Ann Soforth, are the lost king and queen of the kingdom of Oogaboo."

The color drained from the old man's face. "But, but… H-how?"

"I'll tell you how—"

"You named it The Wayward bloody Crowns, you daft old fool!" cut in the head of Nick Chopper with a hearty guffaw. "I'd throw my head back in laughter if I could."

"Nick!" Alaxis chided him.

"'Throw my head back,' says I." And he laughed some more. "Just a bit of dismembered humor, is all."

Alaxis rolled her eyes. "As if you have any other kind."

"You could've done a better job choosing new names for yourselves as well," said the cloaked man to the innkeeper. "It was the 'JJ' that did it for me. But your secret is safe with us." He placed a hand over his heart. "Now how about those drinks?"

JJ scurried over to pour out three glasses. He set one in front of Alaxis, slipped a straw into the second and placed it carefully before Nick, then slid the third to the man tucking the coin purse back into his cloak.

"Thank you kindly," he said as he raised the glass to his lips. And with a wink and a finger to the side of his nose, he placed the glass down and the secret was sealed. "My name," he went on, "is Ku-Klip."

The innkeeper's eyes darted again towards the table at the back of the room where a lone figure sat in darkness. "Master Klip, the mechatronicist and creator of the Tin Woodman?"

"Bucket of bolts who thinks he's me," grumbled Nick between sips, for his head once belonged to the Woodman before he was tin. "I'd headbutt a dent in his shin if I saw him."

"And why I ever kept you around, I'll never understand," Ku-Klip shot back at the head on the bar. "Yes, the Tin Woodman and many more. Many more…" His eyes grew distant as he sipped from his glass.

Just then, Alaxis gestured toward Sandy, who'd been lurking behind a scowl at the end of the bar. The woman strode over and folded her arms across her chest. "JJ'll refill your drink if that's what you're looking for."

"No, ma'am," said Alaxis timidly. "I couldn't help but admire your nail color. Do you think it would look nice on me?" She stretched her shiny copper fingers out toward the woman, their delicate internal pistons extending and retracting as she wiggled them playfully.

The woman cocked an eyebrow and leveled her gaze up at Alaxis.

"It's just…you know, they're new to me, my hands. I just love them." Her cheeks flushed. "And I've never seen nails painted like yours."

Sandy's face softened a bit. "Well, just you sit right there and old So'on will go get some polish from the back." And the faintest of smiles crept to her lips as she strode off, having used her own name for the first time in years.

Ku-Klip beamed with pride as he looked on, admiring his handiwork and the pleasure it brought to his friend. Nick made a gagging gesture with his straw and rolled his eyes.

So'on returned with a little green bottle and took Alaxis's hands in her own. "Forgive me, girl, but you're a Wheeler, right?"

"No ma'am. Never was one in my mind. I was born that way. No feet, no hands, just wheels. And they never once felt right. I was told my whole life it's just what I was, but in my heart, I knew it wasn't." Alaxis took a breath and released it. "So now, with the help of my friend and benefactor here, I'm transitioning to what I've always known that I am."

"And what is that, dear?"

"Why, human, of course." She smiled down at the old innkeeper, who wrinkled her brow for a moment and cocked her head in thought, then smiled back.

"If you are, then you are," she said. "No one knows our hearts better than we do."

Alaxis beamed.

"I used to be a queen, you know." So'on undid the bottle and began to paint smooth, emerald strokes down Alaxis's copper fingertip. The effect was striking. "But I knew in my heart that I wasn't. That that life was not meant for me. So I left."

"Just like that?"

"Just like that." She brushed on another long, even stroke. "And, after a while, Jol left too. He realized he wasn't what he was supposed to be either."

"A king?" Alaxis asked.

So'on shook her head. "A man without me by his side." She glanced up at Alaxis and winked.

"So, Master Klip, you say you're to meet someone here," the innkeeper, Jol, continued, red-faced and pretending he hadn't overheard. "Did you receive a message from him, by chance?"

"I was sent this note to meet here as soon as possible. 'A matter of life and death,' it said." He brushed his beard aside to reach beneath his cloak and drew out a small white card. "It's marked at the bottom with quite a unique symbol, as you can see here."

He handed the card to the innkeeper, who brought it close to his eyes. "I see. Three lines intersecting. An asterisk, is it?"

"The K and K-reversed, fused at the uprights. My maker's mark." He narrowed his eyes. "Not a thing known to many people. It's what led me to believe the message was credible. And that, in turn, is what led us to your door."

Upon inspecting the card, Jol turned toward the table at the rear of the inn and, raising the note between two fingers, nodded to the figure sitting in the shadows. "Apologies, Master Klip, but we had to be sure."

"A rolly girl with clockwork hands and a head in a birdcage weren't proof enough, eh?" shot Nick. "But a paper card with a scribble at the bottom? Well! Must be the right guy!"

"I was told to ask about the note," Jol replied levelly. And as the figure off in the shadows rose from his seat, the innkeeper directed the newcomers toward the back of the inn.

Ku-Klip drained what was left in his glass and lifted Nick's carrier up off the bar by its brass ring, while the straw slipped out from between Nick's lips and plinked back into the glass. "Hey, I wasn't finished with that!"

"Well, carry it over to the table with you, then. Oh, right…" Ku-Klip smirked and followed Jol to the back.

"I'd give you a real piece of my mind if it wasn't all I had left."

"Hat stand."

"Butcher."

The two shared a laugh.

"Now boys…" Alaxis scolded them. She thanked So'on for the polish and the chat, and the two clasped arms before she rolled off to follow her companions.

The figure at the table emerged from the shadows just as Ku-Klip arrived. He pulled back his great grey hood to reveal the chiseled face of a mountain Nome. "Well met, Master Klip. I am Kaliko, as I'm sure you've deduced. Thank you for coming all this way to meet us."

"'Us?'" Ku-Klip asked as he clasped the Nome's outstretched hand.

"Well, yes. Myself and my companion here. He's much worse for wear, I'm afraid, but I do believe—unless I'm very much mistaken—that the two of you have…er…*met?*" The Nome gestured to a chair behind him, set back in the shadows. Sat upon it was a slate grey sack, uncinched at the top and opened enough to reveal its contents, which consisted of every manner of gizmo and gyro, piston and pinion, click spring and crank pin, each one piled upon the next, with a great copper head peeking out from the top.

"G-greetings," it said in a raspy, unoiled tone.

The color drained from Ku-Klip's face as he dropped to his knees, eyes wide. Nick Chopper clanged to the table and had the sense to stay silent for once. Shuffling forward, Ku-Klip gently placed a hand to one side of its pale copper cheek, staring deep into unblinking eyes. "My s—"

he whispered, and the words died on his lips. Ku-Klip rounded on Kaliko. "Who did this to him?"

Kaliko met his glare with a sorrowful look. "My master, Ruggedo the Nome King. He bashed him with a mace and bade me discard the pieces, but I…I just couldn't bring myself to do it."

"And I'm g-glad of that, I don't m-mind saying," creaked the copper man's voice from the top of the sack.

"This tale has one too many talking heads in it for my liking," Nick stated flatly.

"Of all the impertinent…" Alaxis smacked his brass carrier with the back of her hand. Then, turning to Ku-Klip, she asked, "Just who is he, though?"

"I am Tik-Tok of Oz, singular miraculous creation of the great f-firm of Smith & Tinker, friend to Dorothy, s-slayer of witches, first a-and only of my kind." If a dismantled sack of parts could look proud, this one surely did.

"And with Smith and Tinker both long since gone," the Nome continued, "and without the proper skills to help Tik-Tok myself, I had all but lost hope of getting him fixed. Until I found this amongst his pieces." Kaliko reached into his pocket and pulled out a small curved plate with four screw holes in its corners. And there on its coppery surface, etched in three neat crossing lines, was the mirrored K mark of the master mechatronicist, Ku-Klip. "But what I couldn't understand was just how it came to be there. There's no doubt he's a Smith & Tinker marvel; he says so himself. So how came your mark to be etched in his workings?"

"A v-very good question, I th-think. My workings are my own, and I've n-never known I was marked within. But y-your face… there is something… f-familiar."

Ku-Klip sighed and rose. "A tale we may get to in time. As for now, I'm glad to see you've kept his speaking and thinking keys wound. As for the third key, do you have it with you? Not that it's of any use in his present state."

"I have them all here." He produced the three keys from a pouch on a string around his neck and handed them over.

"Jol Jemkiph, a room, sir."

The innkeeper hopped into action and led the way up a rickety stairway to a room at the end of the upstairs hall. The group all followed behind—Master Klip clutching Tik-Tok's sack tight to his chest, Kaliko next, then the tall Alaxis with Nick in her green-polished grasp rolling carefully up each step, and even the kindhearted So'on Ann trailing behind with an armload of everything she could grab that might be of use.

The murmuring patrons and tink-plucking melody rose up the steps behind them, fading off as they stepped through the door. The room was cozy: a neat little bed, a washstand, a desk, and a long-leafed fan on a pulley and gear to ward off the heat of the day.

Ku-Klip strode to the desk and placed the large sack on its surface. He slipped out the keys and wound Tik-Tok's thinking and speaking mechanics for good measure. Then, paying no mind to anyone else, he placed a hand once again to Tik-Tok's smooth cheek and, with a tender, reassuring smile, began to sort parts.

So'on tossed all she'd brought with her onto the bed and slid a small nightstand over to the desk. She laid out an assortment of carpenter's tools, most of which would be useless for such precise and exacting work, but which were offered with the kindest intentions.

Hands on his shoulders, Alaxis loomed over Ku-Klip, intent on witnessing each step of the process, just as she had when she'd gotten her hands. And while Jol returned back to his patrons downstairs, Kaliko paced across the floorboards from one side of the room to the other.

The parts all catalogued and arranged, Ku-Klip slid a hand beneath his cloak and, tossing the length of his beard over a shoulder, produced a tied canvas roll from somewhere on his person. Placing it on the only space left on the desk that was clear of copper bits and bobs, he gently untied its string and rolled it out flat to reveal dozens of sewn-in pockets holding the tools of his trade. Eyeing them up and down, he selected the one he needed and began.

"Smith & Tinker…" Ku-Klip said after a while, his words breaking the silence as his hands continued working. "Smith & Tinker took much of the credit for their apprentices' original designs. You should know that without the least bit of doubt." He spoke to all gathered but addressed Tik-Tok directly. "Not that they weren't strictly entitled to anything and everything designed and created under their roof, for of course they were, as the terms of apprenticeship clearly state. They even affixed a card to his back stating *All infringements will be promptly Prosecuted according to Law*. But to claim their own brilliance, their own hands, were responsible for the work, and keeping the identities of the rightful creators concealed from the public, well…" He wiped the sweat from his smooth round head. "It was an indignity that just could not be borne."

"Charlatans," muttered Nick from a shelf where So'on had resettled him. "I have no stomach for it." He scanned every face for a reaction to his quip, despite its regrettable timing. He got none.

"Brash and brazen were Smith and Tinker," Ku-Klip continued. "Always out in the public eye touting their grand achievements"—he gestured at Tik-Tok—"to the point where they'd gained a cult-like following amongst the citizens, rivaling only the Wizard in some corners of Oz, if you can believe it."

Alaxis's eyes widened, clearly hearing the story for the first time. The parts laid out before Ku-Klip slowly dwindled as they found their way back to their rightful places within Tik-Tok's inner workings.

Kaliko had ceased his pacing to watch and listen. He'd come a long way to hear this story, and his eyes locked in on Master Klip in anticipation of where the tale was headed. "And you were apprenticed to them, I'm assuming?"

"Indeed, I was. And the true creator of Tik-Tok, as I'm sure you've already guessed."

Tik-Tok's eyes grew large and round—if copper spheres that were already large and round could appear any larger and rounder than they were. "I-I do believe I recall it. My very first w-winding. Before even my speaking or m-moving mechanisms were wound. For a m-moment…it was you."

"Yes. With hair on my head, then, and none on my chin. It was I who first wound your thinking mechanism, and I saw in that moment the spark in your eyes. The understanding." Ku-Klip paused to wipe the corner of one eye. "But no sooner had I wound your other two keys and brought you to life than that Tinker swooped in and whisked you off in triumph. I never even got to hear your first words."

"T-they were '*Tik-Tok*,'" he said with a glint in his eyes. "I could h-hear it in my head, in my ch-chest, in the whole of me. As ever I h-have. The tik and the tok and the whirring and clicking. I c-can not *be* without them; I *am* them. And so I n-named myself."

Ku-Klip leaned his head in to meet Tik-Tok's own, brow-to-brow. And with a hand placed behind his smooth copper dome, he said, "Of course you are, my boy. Of course you are."

So'on put an arm around Alaxis and handed her a handkerchief. Even Nick appeared moved, and not just to a shelf.

"Now, let's get you buttoned back up and wind that third key."

As the last light of day filtered in through the window and set into dusk, Ku-Klip completed this wondrous feat, a miracle of mechatronics that hadn't been performed since he'd done it himself all those many years ago. And when he was down to one last part, he ran his finger across his maker's mark and returned it to its place deep within Tik-Tok's chest where a person's heart would reside.

"How do you feel?" asked Alaxis.

"I d-don't *feel*," the copper man replied. "Not as you do. But I am c-complete again. And I am g-glad of that." He bent his elbows and knees to test his joints, which creaked and groaned from the effort.

"It's quite alright, my boy," Ku-Klip offered as he applied oil from a tiny bottle he produced from his pouch. "I assure you I feel enough for the both of us."

"Th-thank you, my… f-father." And he took the old man's hand in his.

"Now let's get that last key wound so Kaliko can get you back to take revenge on that nasty old Nome King for doing this to you in the first place," So'on cried.

Alaxis nodded. "When he sees you coming, he'll think he's seen a ghost!"

"I-I know I don't feel emotion as you all do," Tik-Tok said as Ku-Klip began winding his key. "Though I suspect I m-may be starting to." Ku-Klip's eyes met his with a smile. "But I do not know v-vengeance, nor shall I seek it of the Nome King, as all has turned out s-splendidly in the end."

And they all agreed that it had.

Ku-Klip returned his tools to their delicate pouch, rolled it up and tied it, then slipped it back into its place beneath his cloak. So'on gathered up the things she'd brought, while Alaxis slid the nightstand to its usual place and helped set the rest of the room to rights.

As they all stepped back down the stairs and out onto the main floor of the inn, Joe Tunes's tinkling melody spread through the room and mingled with the aroma of the evening's stew wafting out from the kitchen.

Jol came around the bar and asked if they'd be interested in a warm meal. As they all heartily agreed, he showed them back to the table at the rear of the room.

Soon, So'on came out with steaming hot bowls and some freshly baked bread, which she set out before them. "Something tells me there's a lot more to your tale than you let on." She flashed a raised brow in Ku-Klip's direction. "As someone who's familiar with leaving one life behind and starting over fresh, it does strike me as odd that you ended your apprenticeship with Smith & Tinker in Evna and travelled all the way to Oz to set up shop on your own."

Ku-Klip's eyes remained fixed on the bowl before him.

"And then Smith and Tinker both disappeared," added Alaxis between bites. "Or so the story was told."

"The timing's a tad suspicious if you ask me," asserted Nick. "Rumor had it that Smith drowned in a picture of a river he painted himself. And old Tinker went up a ladder to the moon and then pulled it up behind him." He arched a brow. "A *ladder* to the *moon*! Rather… uh… curious, wouldn't you say?"

Only a handful of people remained at the inn. A family of four sat eating and chatting near the front window. A grey-haired woman sipped from a steaming hot mug as she read from a tatty old paperback, its pages worn and yellowed and barely still clinging to its spine.

Ku-Klip raised a spoonful of stew slowly to his lips and slurped it down. "Smith and Tinker knew enough people would believe whatever they told them."

"A lie will travel halfway around Oz before the truth can get its boots on." So'on nodded.

"People believed they were the greatest inventors of the age. They'd inflated their reputations to near-mythological proportions. And I knew no one would ever believe a mere apprentice could've designed and built their greatest achievement." Ku-Klip set his spoon to the edge of the bowl with a clink. "Not that I needed recognition—it was never about that. But, as I said before, the injustice could not be borne."

"And the wild stories of their disappearances?" Alaxis asked.

"Their image, their public personae, that was their weakness. And I used it against them. The spreading of lies so outrageous, so astonishing, they couldn't help but be believed. A ladder to the moon—so Tinker! A drowning in a painting—classic Smith! The great inventors going out with such flair, such grandiosity." He glanced down at the table. "But the truth is far less fantastical."

"Let me guess," Nick interjected, "beheadings!"

Ku-Klip dismissed this with a scoff and the wave of an arm. "Let's just say Smith & Tinker's smithing and tinkering days were numbered."

Joe Tunes sat at his tink-plucker, the old hollow instrument echoing throughout the room as he plucked its long, metal tinks, each one tuned to a different length and affixed over its oblong soundhole. He deftly plucked out the ending to a wistful, melodic tune, and just as the last notes faded, took up again in a darker, more somber chord.

"And the wild tale of moon ladders and painted rivers"—the corner of Kaliko's mouth rose as he slowly shook his head—"seems to have stuck."

"Then you skedaddled on out of there," So'on added.

"They'd sold my precious Tik-Tok to the King of Ev. What was left for me there? They'd been working on shoddy, inferior designs. A great metal oafish monstrosity that smashed things with a hammer and wasn't even granted the ability to think or to speak." He ran a hand down his beard. "I knew there was nothing left for me there. Nothing to learn from them, no skills left to hone that I couldn't do just as well on my own—if not better. And I knew Smith & Tinker would never again rise to the height of achievement they'd known with Tik-Tok, because I'd vowed never to create for them again."

"And you made certain they'd never prey on another young apprentice like they'd done to you." Kaliko rose and pulled his hood up over his head, then thanked the innkeepers for the meal.

Ku-Klip nodded solemnly and stood. "They…mistreated us. The conditions…they were…poor. They forced us to produce, to create, to design, to build. And those who fell behind…they…weren't apprentices long." His gaze drifted off. "And of course they couldn't send them away and risk word getting out of what truly went on under their roof…"

The words he left unsaid trailed off in a silence that mingled with the mournful dirge drifting out through the inn.

"I am g-grateful for all you've g-given me. For all that you've done." Tik-Tok turned to face his creator. "You were right to d-do what you did. No one d-deserves to be tr-treated that way."

To a person, those gathered nodded gravely in assent.

Ku-Klip's eyes drifted back into focus, and he smiled down tenderly at Tik-Tok. "Never forget, no matter how far your travels take you, no matter where you may find yourself, a part of me is always with you." He patted his bright copper chest plate.

"You've l-left a mark on me far g-greater than the one you've etched w-within my workings." Tik-Tok placed a hand over his chest and bowed. "I will ch-cherish this day as much as I ch-cherish my first. *Our* first." He turned toward Alaxis and took her clockwork hands in his own, looking down at them and turning them over in his copper fingers. "So e-elegant, so fine." He looked up to meet her eyes. "J-just like you."

Alaxis smiled as the color rose to her cheeks. "Safe travels, my friend."

The clockwork man nodded. And, turning toward the innkeepers, he thanked them for their kindness and hospitality. Kaliko wound his three keys as far as they'd go and returned them to the pouch around his neck. Then Tik-Tok, the singular marvel of mechatronics, led his faithful companion out the door of The Wayward Crowns and into the night.

"I like that bucket of bolts. He's got a good head on his shoulders." Nick grinned.

"Yes, he does," Ku-Klip agreed. "And it's time we were off as well." He clasped hands with Jol Jemkiph and So'on Ann Soforth, once rulers of an entire kingdom, now living their best lives as JJ and Sandy, keepers of a quaint little inn.

Alaxis drifted over to So'on and smiled down at the kindhearted woman. "Thank you for seeing me for who I am. And for making me…beautiful." She wagged her emerald green fingertips, and the two exchanged a fond embrace. "You'll always be a queen to me, Your Majesty."

"Oh, none of that, dear. If you'll see *me* for who *I* am, let it always be Sandy."

"Sandy, then." Alaxis nodded and, turning toward Ku-Klip, raised her friend up into the harness behind her.

Handing Nick in his brass-framed carrier back up to Alaxis, Jol met Ku-Klip's eyes and placed a finger gently to his nose. Ku-Klip returned the gesture.

Many secrets were told that night. And many secrets would be kept. With nary a word needed, they all agreed it would be so.

And the dark of the night outside saw a fearsome silhouette framed within the light of the doorway of The Wayward Crowns, which closed behind them—along with this little-known tale of a clandestine meeting at the inn at the edge of Oz.

MASTER CRAFTSMAN
Dennis K. Crosby

The only thing that kept Bevel McCordle wearing blue was his fear of the Wicked Witch of the East.

Bevel didn't hate the color, mind you. He was just so tired of it. Each and every day he'd put on blue pants. A blue shirt. Hat. Shoes. It was all just so…much…blue. Sky blue. Sea blue. Fire blue. Berry blue. Every shade was welcomed with open arms. He once asked if he could try purple. It was, in his mind, close to blue. Sure, there was red mixed in, but still, blue was a part of its essence. Sadly, even that was forbidden. He'd begged. Pleaded, even. But to no avail.

The other Munchkins didn't mind. At least, the elder Munchkins. They wore blue out of tradition. A long and proud tradition. That's what they'd say when questioned about it. It was almost as if they'd forgotten it had been forced upon them.

Did they forget there were other colors?

Bevel certainly didn't, and neither did others of his generation. He didn't want the color banned or outlawed. He just wanted the option of wearing something different. He wanted the option to express himself in a way that was special to him. There was something about the freedom to dress as one pleased that appealed to him.

Bevel was especially upset after he found a hidden closet in the home of the Wicked Witch. It was filled with color. She hadn't worn any of it, of course. He suspected it was color she'd stolen from Munchkins in the past. Before she decreed that blue would be the color of her land.

He'd heard stories of the richness of florals and earth tones among the garb of the Munchkins. It was hard to believe now. Bevel was certain others would stand with him against her if they could see the treasure of color she hoarded in her home.

They never would, of course, for few Munchkins were ever allowed there. Bevel had access because he'd done work there. He'd practically built the place—or rebuilt, as it were. He was a skilled craftsman. In fact, he was among the finest craftsmen in all of Oz. He created beautiful chairs, tables, and such from the wood of the forest. Bevel's talent was so amazing that many thought he was a magician himself. He took great pride in his creations, and though word of his talents spread throughout the land, no one knew his real name. He was only known as the Master Craftsman.

The Wicked Witch saw to that.

She'd cast a spell far and wide that kept anyone from learning about Bevel. As far as anyone knew, there was a Master Craftsman somewhere, but with no name or land of origin, most just chalked it up as legend. Such was the power of her spell. Bevel's talents were simply a tale whispered on the winds of the northern, southern, western, and eastern lands. Residents of Emerald City dismissed such wild claims because surely anyone that skilled would live within their borders. Who wouldn't want to live in the Emerald City? It was the center of…well…everything.

Bevel never dared to ask the witch why she'd cast such a spell.

One day, though, while the witch was speaking with another about a deal to keep someone from marrying, she happened to mention Bevel's work. She spoke of it when portions of the witch's cottage were complimented. Bevel had been working on a cabinet at the time, and overheard.

"Oh my, what lovely furniture you have here," said the woman to the witch. "Did you make it with your powerful magic? It's so…so…fantastic. I've not seen anything like it in all my years."

"I work with the Master Craftsman," said the witch in a moment of vulnerability.

"*The* Master Craftsman?!" said the woman. "He's *real?* They say he makes the finest wood works in all the land! I hear even the Wizard covets his work."

"He does indeed," said the witch. "But no one shall have access to his talents except me. Not even the so-called great and powerful Wizard of Oz."

It was then that Bevel knew he was special.

It was also then that Bevel became determined to leave his fellow Munchkins and travel to the Emerald City to practice his trade. He had family, and many friends, and he would miss them terribly. But he wanted a chance to prove himself, to share his gift beyond his own borders, and to take his rightful place as the Master Craftsman everyone believed was just a legend.

Most of all, he could finally wear something other than blue.

"I'll get there," Bevel said to himself. "I'll get there, and I'll be the best in all the land. I just need to figure out how."

"Just a little more sanding here," said Bevel. He blew away the excess wood dust and ran his finger along the groove of the wardrobe he was building for the Wicked Witch of the East.

It was grand. His finest piece of work by far. It stood just a little taller than the witch herself, and had a steepled top. Two doors opened outward, and below them was a large drawer that pulled open for more clothes or linens and blankets and such.

Bevel had carved wonderful designs into the wood. Images of the forest. Of trees. Bushes. Flowers. It was, in a word, magnificent.

He stood back and admired his handiwork. He wanted to make sure everything worked before taking it inside the witch's cottage. Bevel had been forced to build it outside. The Wicked Witch would not abide a mess in her home.

Bevel pulled the drawer out on the bottom, and it moved smoothly.

"A perfect glide," he said.

He smiled widely and felt the swell of pride in his chest at a job well done.

"Now, the doors," said Bevel.

He opened the right door, then closed it. Not a squeak or a tweak to be heard. Bevel then opened the left door, and it, too, was smooth. Not a squeak or a tweak was heard. He did, however, want to sand the edge just a little more, for his keen eye saw a slight unevenness. Bevel grabbed the rough paper and ran it over the edge. It only took a minute or two to get it just right. Satisfied, he once again blew away any excess wood dust and pushed the door. But something blocked it from closing flush.

"Now that's strange," said Bevel.

He searched all around the outside edges of the wardrobe but saw nothing.

"Hmm," he said. "Maybe the problem is inside."

Bevel opened the doors and stepped inside. He left both doors open wide and examined their interior edges. On the door that worked perfectly, he saw nothing. The other door, though, had a peculiar pebble of some sort stuck on the inside, keeping the door from shutting completely. Bevel placed his finger against it, and it moved.

"Oh my," he said. "That's no pebble. That's a bugaboo."

Bugaboos were harmless. They lived everywhere and nowhere, simply taking up space where they could. When they settled on a spot, they would form a little shell around themselves and stay. They were quite remarkable. They could do it on the ground, a leaf, a wall, a tree…anywhere they desired. A bugaboo only wanted to rest someplace cool and shady. They were greatly attracted to wood—for what reason, no one really knew. They didn't feed on it like other bugs and creatures. They were not a destructive breed, these bugaboos. In this instance, though, they were a bit of a nuisance.

"Oh, my little friend," began Bevel, "Wherever did you come from?"

Bevel, being the gentle soul that he was, stepped out of the wardrobe and grabbed a scrap of wood. He went back inside the wardrobe and pushed the bugaboo onto the new piece.

"There you are, little one," said Bevel. "Let's get you to a new space."

Just as Bevel was about to step out of the wardrobe, he heard a scream of great wind. None of the trees or leaves moved, though. Uncertain of what was coming, Bevel stepped back inside the wardrobe and closed the door.

"I'll just stay here until the wind dies down," he said.

Bevel wasn't afraid, though it may have been smart to be. His little heart did beat faster at the noises he heard. He felt the wardrobe rock a little bit as the wind picked up.

Suddenly, there was a great sound.

POP!

Looking through the slit between the two wardrobe doors, Bevel saw the Wicked Witch of the East appear out of nowhere. She shuffled about, completely ignoring the wardrobe he'd built for her. She looked altogether unpleasant as she mumbled something under her breath.

Bevel opened the door slightly, prepared to step out, but quickly went back in when he heard her return from her cottage. He watched her through the slit between the doors, and this time he heard her clearly.

"This better be all she needs," said the witch.

"All who needs?" Bevel wondered in his mind.

He saw that she was carrying a jar in her hand. He couldn't tell what it was, but assumed it had something to do with magic and spells. Bevel's mind wondered and wandered in so many directions, but he stopped when she did a curious thing.

"To the Wicked Witch of the West," she said, and she clicked the heels of her silver shoes three times. The shoes lit up. Bevel heard rushing wind again. Seconds later there was another great sound.

POP!

And just like that she was gone.

Bevel was not trained in magic. He couldn't even do a simple card trick like his neighbor did for the children. On one hand, he was glad he couldn't do that trick, for the Wicked Witch hated it when others tried to perform magic in her lands. Even simple illusions were forbidden. No, Bevel was not trained in magic, so he didn't know spells, or potions. But he knew tools. He was the Master Craftsman. A tool didn't need to be a hammer, awl, saw, or woodcarver to be important. Bevel knew how to spot tools—even those of a witch or wizard.

Those shoes were magical tools for the Wicked Witch.

"If I can get my hands on those…I could…I could be free. I could be free and travel to the Emerald City and meet the great and powerful Wizard. All my dreams could come true, and…and…I could wear something more than blue."

For the first time, in a long time, Bevel McCordle, the legendary Master Craftsman, had hope for his future. Excited, he exited the wardrobe and headed home.

Even though it was well known that the citizens of Emerald City wore green, Bevel's mind swirled with visions of other colors, too. He saw reds, yellows, and oranges—colors so incredibly bright and vibrant that he couldn't help but smile at the thought of their beauty and warmth. Their images, in his mind's eye, made him dance around his home and hum a tune.

"All I have to do is get those shoes," said Bevel.

In fairness, Bevel did not care for the magic. He didn't want to be a wizard. He simply wanted to be free of the Wicked Witch and able to do what he loved anywhere in the land. The shoes just happened to be the key. They had to be the source of her power, after all.

"Just a click of the shoes and I can go anywhere," he said.

"Go where?" said a voice.

"Oh," said Bevel, surprised. "I didn't know you were here, Mimzi. You startled me."

"Well of course I'm here, my sweet Bevel. Where else would I be?"

Mimzi was Bevel's grandmother—his father's mother. She had another name, but to Bevel, she was always Mimzi. She'd raised him since he was young, since his father had gone off on a trip to find a way to stop the Wicked Witch. A trip from which he never returned. Bevel still had memories of his father. Wonderful, happy memories. Of his mother, too, who'd died in a terrible accident caused by the witch.

Mimzi had been with him his entire life. She believed in him when he didn't believe in himself. She pushed him to always do his best and to do it with a smile. Mimzi was the reason he had such a sweet soul and took such care in all he did.

He would miss her the most when he left.

"I…I don't know," said Bevel. "I was just surprised, is all. How was your day?"

"Oh, it was fine," said Mimzi. "I picked up some things to make a lovely stew tonight."

"The Gornash Stew?"

"The Gornash Stew!"

"Oh, wonderful!" shouted Bevel. "The perfect way to end my day."

Every Munchkin had a skill. Those that didn't demonstrate a skill simply hadn't developed one yet. It would come in time. It always did.

Bevel found his skill early in life. He first carved a small chest for Mimzi on her birthday when he was only ten years old. He apprenticed with another craftsmen for a short time, but Bevel showed creative skill that had far outshone his master. As gifted as Bevel was with wood, Mimzi was with food. Everything she made was his favorite.

His favoritist, though, was Gornash Stew.

"Did you finish the wardrobe, dear?" Mimzi asked.

"I did. Yes," said Bevel.

"Is it magnificent? Oh, what am I asking? Of course it is. It's no doubt the grandest of all your creations."

"I do love it, Mimzi. I hope the witch does, too."

"Maybe now she'll see fit to letting you travel. To show your talents to others," said Mimzi.

Bevel's tummy fluttered. Should he tell her? Should he tell her about the magical shoes and what they could mean for him? Such knowledge could put her in danger. If the shoes vanished, and he vanished, certainly the witch would come for her.

Maybe…maybe he could take Mimzi with him. They could travel together. He could build her a little inn where she could serve her wonderful dishes. Yes. Yes. That was even better. Then he wouldn't have to miss her. She wouldn't be in danger. Plus, she was his Mimzi. He owed it to her to tell her the truth.

So he did.

"Magic shoes, you say?" Mimzi asked.

"Yes. She appeared out of nowhere and I thought it was just because of her power. But when she left, I realized the truth of it."

"The shoes glowed?" Mimzi asked.

"As bright as the moon," said Bevel.

"And then...*pop*?"

"*Pop!*" repeated Bevel.

"Interesting," said Mimzi. "You know, there was a legend of such shoes. They were said to have great power. But I never thought they were the shoes of the Wicked Witch of the East. I expected them to be made of gold, if they existed at all."

"Indeed," said Bevel. "But don't you see, Mimzi? With these shoes, we could leave this place. We could travel to the Emerald City and live there. We could travel anywhere."

"Oh my," began Mimzi, "That would be something. But how would we live? Surely she would come after us. Or worse yet, she could force us to come back by threatening to harm our friends here."

"But with what power, Mimzi? We would have the shoes."

The rumble in Bevel's tummy, the one that came at the prospect of being free, began to settle. He felt the light dim in his mind as a cloud hung over the gaze he shared with his sweet Mimzi.

"You don't think I can do it, do you?" he asked.

"My dear, sweet Bevel. I believe you can do anything you set your mind to. But this thought, this plan is fraught with danger. You wouldn't know a moment's peace."

"But—"

"Besides, having a dream is one thing," continued Mimzi, "but achieving it with honor is another."

"But she's so...mean. So evil. So—"

"Wicked?"

"Yes," said Bevel, defeated.

"There is a saying in Oz," said Mimzi. "It is a little-known saying, but an important one, nonetheless. Especially in the age of the Wicked Witch."

"What is it?"

"It goes like this," began Mimzi. "Even under the heavy shadow of wickedness, a tiny light can lift you from the darkness, for wickedness cannot last forever."

Bevel sat with that thought for a moment. What was the light? Was he meant to be the light? What did it even mean to be the light? Be a good person? A just person? So many questions ran through his mind. So much that he didn't understand. So much that he wanted to do.

"I just…want to be free," said Bevel.

"I know, my sweet dear," said Mimzi. "And to wear more than blue. You know, your father was the same way. He had many of the same thoughts."

From a bag under the table, Mimzi pulled two boxes wrapped in blue paper. One was small, the other much larger. She handed the small one to Bevel first and said, "Happy birthday."

Bevel smiled and took the box. He tore into the wrapping as he always did, ever since he was small, and opened the box.

"This…this was father's pendant," he said.

In Bevel's hand was a small silver pendant with a chain that his father had worn around his neck for as long as he could remember. It was shiny and reflected the light in a rainbow of colors. His father had said it was part of the skin of an ancient and noble creature of Oz. It was meant to protect and remind anyone who wore it that so long as there was love and goodness in the world, evil would never win.

"He always meant for you to have it," said Mimzi. "He left it with me to give to you when the time was right. I suppose it's been long past that time, though."

"Oh, thank you," said Bevel. He put the necklace over his head and looked down proudly at the pendant about his neck. "I shall wear it forever."

Mimzi then handed Bevel the second box. He couldn't imagine what present would top that pendant, though. Curious, Bevel ripped at the paper just as he had the other box. He opened it slowly, despite his excitement. His eyes widened in joy and astonishment. They welled with tears that did not fall.

It was a new pair of shoes…and they were purple.

The next day, Bevel ventured out to see his friends. He had worked long hours on the wardrobe he'd built for the witch over many days. Now, finally, he could relax until the next project presented itself. He wanted to wear his new shoes. To show them off. To feel alive. Bevel knew his friends would love them. The elders, not so much. They wouldn't hate them. They wouldn't even be mad. They just tended to err on the side of caution when it came to upsetting the Wicked Witch. So Bevel didn't wear them.

But he told his friends about them.

"Are they bright?" asked one friend.

"Do they have buckles?" asked another.

"Ohhhh, are they soft like clouds?" asked still another.

So many questions came to Bevel, and so fast, that he could not help but laugh.

"My friends, my friends," he said, holding up his hands. "I promise I will show them to you one day."

"When?" asked the Munchkin nearest him.

Bevel looked at the sky above. He closed his eyes and felt a gentle breeze across his face, took a deep breath and let it out, then made a silent wish—for freedom from the Wicked Witch. Bevel opened his eyes, looked at each of his friends and said, "When she is gone."

There was no need to elaborate. No name was needed. They all knew. Together, they all looked at the sky, closed their eyes, and Bevel imagined they made the same wish as he.

"But look at this other wonderful gift," said Bevel.

From inside his shirt, he pulled his father's pendant. All Bevel's friends were amazed.

"It's beautiful," said one friend.

"So shiny," said another.

"Wow! I wish I could have something like that," said still another.

"My father wore this every—"

Crack-Boom!

Bevel and his friends jumped up immediately.

"What was that?" he asked.

No one knew. It sounded like an explosion of some kind, but they weren't sure where it had come from. When they all looked up and saw swirling clouds, they knew immediately what was happening. Winds howled. Leaves and flowers flew everywhere.

"It's the witch," said Bevel. "She's coming."

Munchkins scrambled, ducking for cover. They hid behind bushes. Behind houses. Sheds. Under tables. They hid because they knew. They knew that when the Wicked Witch arrived in this way, she was mad.

And nothing good happened when she was mad.

There were several minutes of howling winds before the witch finally appeared in the town square.

POP!

Bevel immediately looked from her face to her shoes, now that he knew what they could do. He wanted them for himself. Not to be powerful, but to be free. In fact, they didn't even need to be *his* shoes. They just needed to not be hers.

"You!" she said, pointing at Bevel with a most unpleasant glare.

Bevel looked around and, in that moment, realized that he'd been the only Munchkin to not scramble and hide. He could see little faces peeking out of windows and from behind homes and trees and through bushes. Bevel didn't blame them, of course. They did as they always do.

"M-m-me?" he said.

"Yes. You. Craftsman," she said. There was a snarl in her voice when she spoke, causing her disappointment to arrive well before her words registered.

"H-h-how may I be of service?" Bevel asked.

"How may you be of service?" she asked.

Her tone was mocking. What could he have possibly done? He'd just finished his finest piece of work for her. Quite possibly the finest piece of woodworking in all the land. How could she be upset?

"You can fix that abomination of a wardrobe you made, Craftsman!"

"Abomin—but it was my finest work," said Bevel. "There's nothing else like it."

"That's a good thing indeed, Craftsman. Because it's awful. Terrible. I wouldn't give that to my worst enemy. And I have plenty," said the witch.

Of that, Bevel was certain.

"But everything about it was perfect," insisted Bevel. "The wood is smooth. Symmetrical. The drawers glide easily. The doors—"

"Don't close!"

"They…don't—but that's impossible," said Bevel. "I checked everything. Double checked. Triple checked. It all worked perfectly."

The witch walked toward Bevel slowly. He tried not to show his fear, but it was hard. The Wicked Witch of the East was terrible. Unpredictable. Especially when she was upset. He was glad he hadn't worn his new shoes. They would have driven her over the edge.

"There was a bugaboo in my wardrobe. You tried to infest my wardrobe and everything I own…with BUGABOOS!"

Bevel shook his head. He whispered, "No," several times before it finally came aloud.

"NO!"

The shock on the witch's face spoke volumes. Bevel looked around and saw the shocked faces of his friends and all the Munchkins hiding in various areas around him. Had he really just yelled at the witch? He hadn't meant to. Had he?

"You. Dare," she said.

Bevel's immediate thought was to fall to his knees in fealty. He worried about himself, sure. More than that, he worried about his friends. About his dear sweet Mimzi. What if the Wicked Witch took out her anger at him…on them? He considered all the possibilities but chose to stand his ground.

Bevel was calm and focused. In a way that he had not been with anyone in a while. In fact, the only time he'd ever been this calm and focused was when he was working. Bevel knew the witch was unpleasant. He knew that it only took the smallest of things to set her off. But Bevel also knew that he was a Master Craftsman. His work was above reproach. And he would allow no one to speak ill of it.

Not even the Wickedest of Witches.

"I mean no disrespect," said Bevel. "But I can assure you, I did no such thing. I admit, when I first tested your wardrobe, there was a problem with one of the doors, and it was, indeed, a bugaboo that caused the malfunction. But the creature was relocated, and everything was as it should be. You have no cause to do this. To come here like this. To scare my friends. We are good people and have done nothing to deserve this."

A deathly silence filled the space between Bevel and the witch. It lasted for only a few seconds, but in those seconds, Bevel aged years. Finally, the silence was broken with a most wicked and terrible laugh. When the witch finally stopped, she stepped back from Bevel and raised her arms high.

Bevel looked at the sky again and saw clouds swirling into a funnel. It was a dark gray mass that spun faster and faster, slowly lowering as the witch lowered her arms.

"Since you tried to destroy my home, I will destroy all of yours!" yelled the witch.

"No! Please!" screamed Bevel.

His words fell on deaf and angry ears. The funnel cloud continued to lower. No longer able to look, Bevel lowered his head. He happened to glance at the silver shoes of the witch and saw that they glowed bright. Lowering his head further, he saw the light reflected in the pendant he wore. He grabbed it and lifted it slightly to say a silent prayer to his father.

"Argh!"

Bevel followed the sound. Looking up again, he saw the witch disoriented from glare. The reflection of her bright shoes in his pendant flashed in her face. Right in her eyes. Her arms flailed to block the obstruction and with her frantic movements, and with their movements, the funnel cloud shifted away.

Bevel breathed a sigh of relief. But it was short lived. For when the witch recovered, her scowl was even more foul than before.

"You think you've won?" asked the witch.

It was clear she didn't want an answer. What she wanted…was revenge.

"I'll simply bring it back and destroy everything!" she shouted.

Just as before, the witch raised her arms, and her shoes began to glow. Within seconds, the funnel cloud returned from wherever it had gone. Only…something was different. The cloud began to fall even before the Wicked Witch lowered her arms. She seemed not to notice, though. Her gaze was fully focused on Bevel. He looked from the cloud to her face, and back again. Now another peculiarity formed within the cloud. An object. A large one. It spun within the funnel. The cloud kept falling. So did the object within. When it was clear that it was about to crash from the sky, Bevel dove for cover.

"Too late for—"

SPLAT!

The Wicked Witch couldn't even finish her sentence. Bevel covered his head to shield his eyes from dirt and wind. When everything died down, he looked up and saw the impossible. Where the witch once stood was a house. From beneath the house, he saw…feet.

He knew whose feet they were when he saw the silver shoes.

As the rest of the Munchkins rose from the ground and emerged from their hiding spaces, Bevel walked over to the house that had fallen from the sky. It was big. Certainly bigger than his own home, or any Munchkin's home, for that matter. It was made of wood. Nothing as lovely as he could make, though. The house was altogether plain. He looked inside a window and saw a little girl sleeping. Next to her was a small hairy black creature with four legs and a tiny tail.

"My word," Bevel whispered. He looked down at his pendant and his Mimzi's words echoed in his brain.

"Even under the heavy shadow of wickedness, a tiny light can lift you from the darkness, for wickedness cannot last forever."

As other Munchkins gathered, Bevel backed away and quickly ran to his home—to put on his purple shoes.

NEITHER OLDER NOR LARGER
Nicole Field

Ozma had been staring silently upon the elegant and extravagant gown made of the weightless silk she most preferred.

"Do you…not like it, Princess?" It was Jellia Jamb who asked the question, her youthful voice tentative. "I can have the seamstress who made it—"

"No need to bother the seamstress," Ozma said with a wave of her hand. She was not rude. She would not be rude to her favorite attendant out of the Emerald City staff. Yet her gaze never left the gown.

Ozma remembered her first time staring upon the splendor of a gown, one belonging to the woman who once had been General of the Army of Revolt. Ozma had thought it such a wonderfully barbaric thing at the time. Certainly, the old clothes with which she'd escaped from the Gillikins and the Witch who had raised her seemed nothing in comparison to the vivid silk costume in emerald green, sapphire blue, citrine yellow, ruby red and, of course, the amethyst purple for Country of the Gillikins.

When General Jinjur had spoken to Ozma of an army composed of girls who stuck into their hair long, glittering knitting needles with which they were to battle, and not an ugly face in the entire army, Ozma had been impressed. No, more than impressed. She had thought a girl must be a wonderful thing to be.

Of course back then, Ozma had been just a boy named Tip. Well, 'Tippetarius,' actually, though no one was expected to say that when 'Tip' would do just as well.

A sigh escaped Ozma now without her realizing it.

"Princess?" Jellia said, drawing Ozma's attention outside of herself once more.

Ozma shook her head.

"The gown will be fine, Jellia," she replied. "Of course it will be fine. That will be all. Please let no one come into my rooms for now."

Jellia nodded her head and stepped back from the outermost of Ozma's rooms until she was in the hallway and closing the door softly behind her.

Without Jellia to watch on her, Ozma stood and walked around her rooms. She brushed her fingers against several ornaments and decorations, as she had once done in the rooms of the Nome King's palace. The ornament of a pretty grasshopper had been the third of the transformations her body had undergone, or so she had understood afterwards.

The idea that had crossed Ozma's mind more than once was that the pretty emerald grasshopper had not been a true transformation of herself, and *that* was why she remembered none of her time in it.

Ozma progressed to her bedroom, and from there towards the window across from the curtains behind which her Magic Picture hung. From this window, she could overlook most of the Emerald City and so many of its citizens going about their days. So much green. She had lived here for years already, but she was always struck by how *green* everything was in the Emerald City, as opposed to the *purple* of Gillikin. Was it homesickness she felt, then? No. Ozma thought she knew herself a little better than that.

Before too long, she had once again found herself lost in thought and, when she looked down to her hands, she was surprised to find them shaking.

Ozma wished to see Dorothy. Oh, how desperately she wished to see Dorothy.

Dorothy lived within the palace of the Emerald City now, along with her Uncle Henry and Aunt Em. Once, Dorothy had told her, they had not believed in the land of Oz. Those days were far behind them now. It was something for Ozma to be grateful of.

Not enough to stop that slight shake, though. She put one hand over the other so she would at least no longer have to look at it.

While Ozma had the tasks she needed to continue doing in order to keep Oz being a most wonderful place no one ever wished to leave, Dorothy had earned similar responsibilities ever since Ozma had raised her to the station of Princess by her side.

Who, other than Dorothy, had done so much for Oz as Ozma?

As though Ozma's thoughts had summoned her, Dorothy entered through the doors to her rooms. It was just as well Dorothy, and Dorothy alone, was one who needed no invitation to come into Ozma's rooms. Otherwise, Jellia could have quite simply turned her away.

"What is this I'm hearing about none being admitted into your rooms?" Dorothy asked, her fair head turning to one side in curiosity.

Ah. So Jellia *had* attempted to make Ozma's wishes known, even to Dorothy.

And then, because it was Dorothy, and Ozma couldn't hope to keep anything from her, Ozma turned from her window with the lovely and welcoming smile for which she was perhaps most known.

"Well, hello dear." Ozma said. She took both of Dorothy's hands in her own and brought her close for a kiss. Only afterwards did she note her hands were no longer shaking. "What beautiful timing you have. I was just looking for a reason to escape…" Ozma didn't wish to reveal, all of a sudden, the reason for her disjointed and messy thoughts.

Yet Dorothy's expression began to turn confused the longer Ozma's silence stretched on.

"… the Wizard!" she concluded in a rush. The Wizard *had* come to her earlier that morning, some hours ago now. It worked as a convenient enough excuse.

"Oh?" Dorothy asked, as Ozma relinquished her only so far as a handspan away. "And what terrible thing has he requested of you today?"

Ozma allowed herself a long sigh. "Well. Apparently there is word from Ruggedo, the former Nome King. You remember. He wishes to speak with me. About a *favor.*" Unconsciously, Ozma's fingers found and began to lightly stroke the Magic Belt that had formed such a point of contention between herself and the former ruler.

Unaware of it, Dorothy's eyes only widened in a mimicry of Ozma's own. "And what is this favor?"

Ozma should have known Dorothy would ask. Although Ruggedo *had* been an adversary several times in the past, he'd also been lately quite successful in not returning to patterns of enslavement, invasion and conquest, owing to his continued stay under Ozma's watchful eye and within the Emerald City.

So Ozma shook her head. Her interaction with the Wizard had quickly ceased to be a useful diversion. "I do not want to talk about favors today." Hoping to distract her dearest friend, Ozma linked her arm with Dorothy's and started them both walking into one of the sitting rooms outside of where she slept. "I wish instead to talk about time."

"Time?" Dorothy asked.

"And aging," Ozma added, as though it had been an afterthought.

It had *not* been an afterthought.

Yet Dorothy answered exactly as Ozma had expected her to. "But aging hardly happens here in Oz!"

"Does it not?" Ozma tilted her head as though Dorothy had just said the most curious thing. "Once, the people of Ev could not believe it was possible for animals to talk, or of such tales as those of the Tin Woodman or the Scarecrow. Tell me, do see me as your same age, or older when you look at me now?"

"I see you as… Oh! Older, I think." Dorothy sounded unsure even as she spoke the words, looking directly into Ozma's eyes but also squinting as though this couldn't possibly be the correct answer.

Because, as they both knew, that had not been the case when they'd first met.

Dorothy had recounted to Ozma her first memories of seeing the Princess of Oz in the foreign land of Ev. Dorothy had told Ozma that her first impressions had been that she was beautiful. A beautiful girl in a beautiful chariot with a beautiful diadem across her forehead. A girl who was neither older nor larger than her.

And Ozma had her own first memories of Dorothy besides. As Ozma had watched on, the Scarecrow—who had been king of Oz by the time Ozma first arrived—gently advised Dorothy she might feel safe even despite her imprisonment. Ozma remembered the way the corners of her lips had quirked to see these two friends reunited.

Stories of their adventures had already grown into legend before Ozma had ever taken over rulership of Oz.

Then Dorothy's eyes had moved to Ozma's for the first time…

In the personages of both Tip and Ozma, she had experienced both the kindness and the cruelty of Oz. She had come to Ev only to discover the same thing was true in that land. Truly, Ozma no longer believed that kindness could exist without cruelty standing right beside it. Certainly not without a great deal of effort on the part of the ruler of any great place.

But, when Dorothy had looked back at her, Ozma had seen only kindness. Though she had looked, there had not been anything but matter-of-factness and curiosity alongside the kindness in her eyes. And Ozma had been smitten.

Dorothy had equally admitted to the knowledge that she would learn to love Ozma dearly. Never a day spent in each other's company had shown either one of them that their initial instincts had been wrong.

However it was presently *now*, not *then*, and Ozma was not done with her questions in the present.

"Further, do you see before you a boy child named Tip?" Ozma pressed.

"I do not," Dorothy had to say.

And that, right there, was the problem, wasn't it?

Ozma's shoulders hunched, but she only nodded, as though this had answered everything she'd initially wished to prove.

"Before you began to live in Oz, how did your continued visits here and to the surrounding lands start?" Ozma asked next. "Was there always a cyclone present?"

"Goodness, no."

"No tossing of waves to send you overboard?" Ozma lifted her eyebrows innocently enough, though she knew of course the answer Dorothy would make.

"I told you already, no!"

"No sights or sounds of any earthquake?" Ozma bit her lip subtly as she asked this question.

"Of course not!"

"Magic means, then. What about Silver Slippers?" Ozma asked and then, when Dorothy only shook her head in astonishment, she added, "My Magic Carpet?"

"Ozma! *What* is this about?" Dorothy demanded suddenly, and with a single quick stomp of her slippered foot.

Ozma placed both her hands on her hips and took a deep breath, steeling herself even as she stared unrelentingly at Dorothy. "Just ensuring you can admit to how things *can* change here."

"Of course I do," Dorothy huffed, because Ozma had given her very little other choice.

"I find I no longer wish to be so unchanging, Dorothy Gale," Ozma said heavily. "Not anymore."

"I see," Dorothy said. And then, being ever of a curious nature, she added only, "How can I help?"

Ozma had to admit, she'd not believed things would move along so smoothly as this. For a moment, she only stared at her friend in a rare moment of having no idea of what to say. And then she regathered herself.

"Could you try something for me? Only something very little. I want to see what happens if you try to change your age," Ozma said. Then, as Dorothy began to show alarm, she added, "The aging spell my mother put in place still stands. You will only age as much as *you* wish, I promise. A year, perhaps two or three. And, as you try, I will watch carefully to see if I can take note of the way it looks."

It was possible there was a way other than utilizing the Magic Belt for Ozma to succeed in what she wished to attempt. She had always used her fairy powers to make *other* people happy. Truly, Ozma knew that was the only way for a princess so powerful as her not to be miserable.

Yet, of late, misery had been finding her anyway. Was there such a difference between the absence of pleasure found when gaining something too easily versus the absence of pleasure due to the loss of a part of oneself?

It *would* be selfish to use the Magic Belt knowing, as Ozma did, that it only allowed the wearer one wish per day. Yet the Magic Belt had become a regular part of her wardrobe. Wearing it as she so often did, Ozma had been unable not to think of late about the other possibilities it might afford her.

She *can't* be selfish in this. All of Oz look to her to be their kind and just ruler! How would it look if anyone were even to know of how she considered using the Magic Belt to her own advantage?

Ozma found her breath coming to her faster than was useful.

"Are you quite alright?" Dorothy asked, seeming to notice that not all was well with Princess Ozma of Oz.

"Will you do it?" Ozma asked instead of answering. Then, softening her words, she reached out to touch the back of Dorothy's hand lovingly. "Will you try this for me, my dear?"

Dorothy's lips parted. Then, "Of course," she said gently. The hand that Ozma wasn't already holding came up to rest over both of their hands. Ozma felt her shoulders loosen, if only a little, at this evidence of Dorothy's ongoing affection. "You know I would do anything for you."

Ozma nodded only once. She did not trust herself to speak and so only watched as Dorothy closed her eyes.

And then, as she watched, Dorothy slowly aged before her very eyes.

It was not a great deal. One to three years, as Ozma had suggested. Dorothy's blonde hair grew longer, though it maintained its curls. Her arms and legs grew, as did the nails on her slightly longer, more delicate fingers. Dorothy's face was still her face, but it was altered also in a way that seemed natural yet stole Ozma's breath at the same time. There was definition to Dorothy's cheekbones and jawline that had not been there before.

Ozma must have let out a gasp, because Dorothy suddenly opened her eyes. Behind those eyelashes, though, Dorothy's eyes were still exactly the same.

"Oh!" Dorothy said, pulling her hands away from Ozma and looking down at herself. "It seems I was not finished growing yet." The skirt she had worn was now several inches above where it had been, causing both

Dorothy and Ozma to laugh at this unexpected side effect. And that was how Ozma realized that both Dorothy's voice *and* her laugh had changed ever so slightly to suit her new age.

"Here," Ozma said, reaching out to pick up a reflective glass and passing it to Dorothy. An expression of shock and surprise took over Dorothy's face as she took in the differences Ozma had already seen.

Ozma ended up distracted despite herself. While Dorothy still gazed at herself, Ozma considered all she'd seen. The aim must be to let this transformation happen slowly, she decided. And then to discover whether that transformation could be made to include another form that had once also been hers.

"All right," Ozma said quietly, as if to herself. As if it wasn't what all of this had been leading to. As if she wouldn't be completely shattered if she was unsuccessful. "My turn."

She couldn't quite meet Dorothy's eyes again after that. She believed she would lose her nerve entirely if she tried. Closing her eyes, then, Ozma was careful *not* to make a wish, mindful that she still wore the Magic Belt around her waist. This was not a wish. This was merely directing the spell her mother had once cast over all of Oz.

Age, she willed herself. *Age as Tip would have done.*

Despite the hope she had felt from the moment she'd decided to explore this possibility, Ozma hadn't truly been certain it was something she could actually do. It was something, in fact, that Glinda the Good had stated *she* could not do, being that Glinda never dealt in transformations.

Yet the thought had kept coming back to her: Ozma was descended of the individual who had paused aging and death for any and all in Oz. What was that except a transformation of every man, woman, child and other creature living in Oz?

Transformations had only seemed to become more common since Ozma's ascension to ruler. Ozma had not even *known* about the Magic Belt back then.

Ozma hesitated to open her eyes even as her fingers once more touched against the familiar metal of the Magic Belt. There was no sound from Dorothy, no noise at all to indicate whether Ozma had been successful in what she'd attempted to do.

No indication as to whether she would feel pulled to use the Magic Belt, despite what she felt about using magic of any sort to provide one's own needs and wants.

But then, she gathered her courage. She had not even the excuse of the Cowardly Lion, who himself had battled and overcome his cowardice multiple times for the good of all of Oz.

Ozma, *and* Tip, could be proud to follow in that example.

"Oh." The word was a mild exclamation, voiced not long after he opened his eyes. In fact, it wasn't an exclamation at all, so much as a sound of mild observation. Only on the inside of his chest did Tip's heart suddenly feel as though it was darting around like an uncivilized rabbit. If there had been a test to find himself again, then he had passed it.

Maybe that test had only been in his own mind.

This was him, then. No need at all to utilize the Magic Belt. This was himself as he would have been, had he never agreed to return to the guise of Ozma.

He'd thought, for a long while after that, that the dissatisfaction he felt within himself was something to do with what he'd grown up knowing against what was arguably now the truth of who he was. Princess Ozma of *all* of Oz! Not merely Tip, the orphaned child of Gillikins. Who would not wish to make that transformation? He should have been grateful!

Tip had tried to look at his new self the same way everyone else had seemed to. He'd tried to press all that wonder and delight into himself.

And, sometimes, it even worked. On those days, Ozma would smile and stand confidently in the Throne Room while ensuring all her people had every one of their needs met. She would walk out into the various lands of Oz along with the Wizard, or Dorothy, at her side and she would ensure all wrongs were punished and all rights rewarded.

Yet always, inevitably, it had come back to him eventually the feeling that he was an imposter living within his own skin. That had been the problem today when he'd been faced by Jellia Jamb and the gown. That had been what made him freeze rather than accept this newest garment with delight.

He didn't have to go through that any longer, though. Because *this* could be him.

Tip realized, all of a sudden, that he was staring overmuch at the back of his browned hand. He turned it around before clenching it into a fist and then flexing it out again. His skin was as brown as he remembered it from childhood. His forearms were strong, owing to the strenuous work that had so often required of him by the old witch, Mombi.

But they were *his*. The sight of every part of himself again took his breath away.

Tip remembered the moments right before Mombi returned him to the form of Ozma under Glinda's determined command. Tip had looked at the Scarecrow, the Tin Woodman, and the other friends he'd made before asking, *"I hope none of you will care less for me than you did before. I'm just the same Tip, you know; only—"*

His words had failed him then. It had seemed as though his friends had understood. And he knew they loved him still. He knew that.

Yet *they* saw only Princess Ozma when they looked at him now.

Something very important had been taken away from Tip that day. Something disregarded as his friends had made their plans to place him on the throne. Tip had been so young, then, too young to understand it properly.

He'd learned how to understand things better now.

He only belatedly remembered he was in the same room with someone else, and that that person was *Dorothy*. Tip turned his attention to his dearest friend and found her staring down at his hands exactly as he had just been.

Dorothy had told Ozma before that her first impressions had been that she was beautiful. And so Ozma had thought it was important to Dorothy that Ozma was beautiful. Yet the way Dorothy now gazed with appreciation at the strength evident in Tip's hand and arms had Tip reconsidering something *he'd* previously thought he knew.

Eventually, Dorothy's eyes lifted to find his. Her smile, when she met his gaze, was as brilliant as any of Ozma's had ever been described.

"Ah," Dorothy breathed eventually, before lifting her hand up to touch the side of Tip's face. Her gaze never moved away from him. "It *is* you. What would you like me to call you now? Tip?" Her voice never raised above a reverent whisper, even as she spoke his other name for the very first time.

Mutely, Tip nodded. Although Dorothy had touched Ozma many times before, her fingertips had never lingered on Tip.

She had never seen *him*. But she saw him now.

Dorothy nodded to herself, not seeming to need Tip to offer any words of reason or explanation.

"These are still the eyes that belong to my dearest friend." Dorothy's voice rose just above a whisper this time. The wonder didn't stay in her voice long past that point. Dorothy had seen too many things in Oz and its surrounding lands for that.

It was only Tip who found himself completely undone. Tip who, he realized now, had almost entirely convinced himself he did not deserve to be *all* of who he truly was.

Oz had grown unused to change. For all its regular visitors from children of the outside world and changes in who ruled this City or that, Oz had become very good at remaining very much the same.

Ozma, as its princess, had always done her best to maintain that status quo. But Tip could not do it anymore. He may have been born a girl child before becoming a boy who had grown into a young man in search of his luck and travelling to the Emerald City. There he'd become not a young man, but a young woman; not an orphaned slave child to old Mombi, but the very ruler of Oz. But that wasn't *all* of who he was.

Both Ozma and Tip were the very definition of change, and so *Oz* needed to become open to a bit more of that again. He would not betray the land of Oz for being his true self. He would betray *himself* if he did not.

In the end, it seemed Dorothy only had one question left.

"But you are not a Wizard or a Witch. You are a Princess. Prince." Dorothy's natural curiosity was back even as she finished this sentence with a small noise of question in the back of her throat, as though she did not wish to accidentally offend by getting it wrong.

And that made Tip relax. Only then did he begin to explain the same thoughts that had so recently occurred to him as a possibility.

Dorothy nodded and stayed silent until Tip had finished articulating how this plan had come to be. Then he'd paused, before admitting his shameful, most selfish secret. "I had thought to use the Magic Belt... if this could not be done in any other way."

Dorothy eyed him sadly with that admission, but she did not judge. Nor did she offer any opinion on the journey he'd undertaken to get to this part of himself again.

When she finally spoke, it was to say, "'When I was a child, I spake as a child, I understood as a child, I thought as a child: but when I became a man...'"

Tip did not recognize the words for himself. Still, it was clear Dorothy had heard them before and that she recited them again now. He thought Dorothy might have been commenting on the way he'd once chosen to become Ozma for no reason other than because he'd been a child then, and he hadn't known better.

Dorothy's words trailed off and her eyes opened incrementally. Still, it was a moment before she spoke again.

"You never became a man," she uttered, far more in her usual tone of voice, but the words themselves rocked Tip to his very core.

"No," Tip answered his voice hoarse. "I chose something different."

"Do you regret that choice now?" Dorothy asked, sounding as though she wanted nothing more than his honest answer.

Did he regret that choice now?

"I don't know," Tip said honestly. Things weren't so simple as that.

"Have you… often wished to return to this form?" Dorothy asked.

"Not… often," Tip answered, careful to be honest with her—with himself—no matter how it might sound. "But sometimes over the years, yes. I thought, at first, I only wished to return to what I had always known."

"And now?" Dorothy asked.

"Now…" Tip pressed his lips together, then squared his shoulders even as it occurred to him he did not need to feel uncertain *or* ashamed of whatever his thoughts were or had been. Not in this space. Not in front of Dorothy. When he spoke again, his words already sounded surer. "Now I know I understand this too is a part of me. I am a girl. At other times, I am a boy. I am both and don't need to content myself with only choosing one or the other."

He smiled affectionately at Dorothy, feeling the truth shining from his eyes like starlight, for it had been such a relief to say these words and to hear them said.

Indeed, it felt as though the sitting room was larger than it had been before. As though the possibilities before him were greater than they ever had been.

He moved then a little closer towards Dorothy, only to hesitate at the last moment. Though it had become common for *Ozma* and Dorothy to greet one another with a kiss, it was just another thing that had never been done between *Tip* and Dorothy.

Tip bit his lower lip, betraying his own uncertainty.

"It's okay," Dorothy said softly, and it struck him again how her voice had also changed somewhat. Maybe not so dramatically as his, but it *was* different. "I cannot imagine there is anything you could do that I would not be just as comfortable with as with the version of you I better recognize."

Tip breathed out slowly as these words lifted a great weight from his mind. "I only wondered if I might offer you a kiss in greeting? Nothing untoward, just—"

Dorothy closed the distance between them. Tip was surprised, but he overcame it quickly. His warm brown hands found the sides of her face and their lips pressed and moved against each other as though they'd always done exactly this. However, it was… dissimilar too. Perhaps owing to Tip's gender though, just as likely, it was also the difference in Dorothy's age.

Dorothy was smiling as she slowly pulled away. She let out an unsteady breath and lowered her eyes demurely before looking up at him again. Tip wondered whether her heart was suddenly beating as rapidly as his, but he didn't ask. Instead, he tried to school his words.

"And now, we have greeted one another once more," he said softly, after a moment of mutual silence between them.

Dorothy laughed, and it was the same laugh as when they'd both realized how her skirt sat differently upon her legs.

"So we have," she said, sounding quite delighted.

Tip nodded to himself before he moved to find the chaise that was his favorite to recline upon when the two of them sat together in this room. And then Dorothy moved to sit comfortably at his feet, in the place where she just as commonly sat with Ozma. There she gazed up at him, and he knew he was still every bit her dearest friend as he had ever been.

And within the pages of the Great Book of Records, it was written:

"When Tippetarius of Oz was in presence, he was both a wise and a wonderful Ruler of Oz. And, when Ozma of Oz was in presence, she was both a wise and a wonderful Ruler of Oz."

THE PURPLE SPIDER GIRL OF GILLIKIN COUNTRY
Jeannie Warner

Reera the Red was wearing her usual gorilla shape high in the treetops of Gillikin Country, looking out over a forest shaded in lavender to deep purple leaves against the brown tree trunks. She was knitting a particularly interesting cable pattern that involved a lot of counting and not at all disposed to receiving visitors, let alone visitors with letters from people. So when the winged monkey flapped down onto the broad branch in front of her where she leaned against the trunk and cleared its throat two or three times, she stared at it, silent. The needles went still in her fingers.

Not finding words in the face of her steady gaze, the monkey cleared its throat again and held out the trifold letter. It was sealed with a bit of magic and a glittering L. Reera was still for a minute, to see if waiting would make it go away, but the creature gamely stood its ground, missive in hand.

"No reply, I trust?" She sighed at last, reaching for the paper.

"No ma'am," the monkey offered with uncharacteristic sobriety and respect. "And I'm to 'hie myself right off after delivery and not do anything I either would or wouldn't regret later,' she says. So. Ma'am." It doffed the little cap, spread its wings, and swooped off into the lower leaf canopy and out of sight.

Knowing of the winged monkeys' penchant for mischief, Reera watched the dot of red cap distrustfully until it disappeared in the distance before sighing and opening the letter. It started baldly, without any niceties or greeting.

> *I need you to visit the purple spiders discreetly. They have a new servant, a Mountaineer, and Herself would be vexed if the girl came to harm. But the earth whispers uncertain things about the girl, and I'd like to know what will happen if I do nothing.*

> *Do this and I will see to it that everyone forgets about that old affair and your meddling. My word and seal on it.*

L

"I want to be left alone, Locasta!" Reera growled, but shifted slightly on her branch. The previous affair mentioned in the letter was not something she wanted to think about, and Mrs. Yoop had done perfectly well in the long term. But the promises of a Cardinal Witch were nothing to sneeze at, and Reera thought Locasta rather the best of the lot. And so, the grey ape in her lace cap slipped her knitting into an apron pocket and climbed down from her favorite afternoon tree.

Once in her meadow, Reera walked through the knee-high purple grasses as her body shrank and transformed into the form of a pretty red-haired human woman outside a small cabin. She wasted little time inside, lingering only long enough to dip her fingers into a small drawer high on a shelf. They curved around a bit of dust, which she extracted and smoothed into the bottom of her apron pocket. She paused at the door, then sighed and strode out into the dappled sunlight through the forest.

The sun was low in the sky when Reera reached the edge of the spider territory, where she paused by a scrap of webbing floating in a light breeze over the path. She lifted a dusty finger to touch it, feeling the silken skein formed inside a fellow living being. It pulsed gently with the knotted weave of a new form, and Reera let her heart beat once more, turning blood to hemolymph by a word given silent shape on her lips. With that internal alteration complete, she let her body flow into the shape of a large purple spider.

Reera preferred most any other form to that of human, and while the purple spider shape was not in her normal rotation, she enjoyed a sudden awareness of the patterns of all the webbing as it slowly collected along the path until it was a tunnel that met others to branch off in three directions. There she stopped and, lifting a front leg, tapped the ceiling of the webbed tunnel three times.

Two purple spiders appeared from different tunnels, creeping low and defensively toward the conjunction point. "Who are you? What do you want?" spoke the larger of the two, and Reera dipped her head and thorax slightly in greeting.

"I am Reera. I will consume no resources and need no mate, but I would like the use of a servant for a short time while I consider an important matter. Do you have a human one I might borrow?"

The two spiders conferred in a quick series of soft clicks and foot movements before allowing that they did have such a servant, and that Reera could indeed borrow her services temporarily. "She is not allowed outside the nests without her anklet," they warned.

"I will not remove it," Reera agreed, and waited while one of the two skittered off down the ceiling of the third tunnel. Some minutes later, a youngish Mountaineer was brought out for inspection, and the Yookoohoo inspected her thoroughly. The human girl was of middling height, dressed simply in a purple gown with bulging pockets and wearing macrame slippers. She had a thick manacle of spider silk around one bare ankle with a long, trailing tether. Her eyes and hair were dark, but Reera marked a glint of purple flash in her gaze when she turned to curtsey to the spiders and again to Reera.

"She will do nicely. Thank you. This way, girl." And with a claw touching the girl's back, she turned and guided her out of the nest.

The girl walked in silence as she was led, and Reera led the two of them to a nearby meadow where only the wisps of old webs drifted idly in the breeze. She folded her legs down and settled into a comfortable hollow. "Sit, girl. Wherever you like. I should like to hear your story."

"MY story?" the girl asked, startled. "Why would you want that?"

"I collect stories. It's the one interesting thing about people. So, tell me about you. Are you happy here? Serving the spiders?"

The girl blinked her confusion. "What an odd question. I suppose so. I'm used to being ordered about, and the spiders are not cruel or unreasonable."

Reera clicked her mandibles once. "Used to it? Were you ordered about back on Flathead Mountain? Or by the Skeezers?"

If the girl was surprised that Reera knew where she had come from, she didn't show it. "Oh, we were all ordered about. I was the Dictator of Scullery there. Just about everyone was more important than me."

"Dictator of… what?"

"Everyone used to be a Dictator," the girl explained. "I used to be something else before that, but…" She sighed and shrugged, scratching at the back of her head, then cupping it. "It's harder to remember what happened after my brains were stolen. I feel like I lost a lot of things that happened there, and I don't really know how much time passed. The Supreme Dictator, or maybe his wife - they had my brain can for a long time. They said I didn't really need it, just tending to the kitchens and sweeping and such. And I supposed I didn't at that. You need more attention than deep thought to get a pot cleaned out proper."

Reera sighed. "This is why I hate people."

The girl looked startled, and there was a momentary glint of fear in her eyes as she sprang to her feet. "You're not going to eat me, are you? They promised me that spiders don't eat anything that talks, so…"

"I'm not going to eat YOU, spider girl," Reera stated quite clearly. "I'm just rather put out with how humans and fairies seem to let all the wrong people run their enclaves. It happens far too often. And thinking is important for everyone. So. Sit down, if you please. Tell me of these deep thoughts you want to think about now. Starting with your name?"

"My name is Landria." The girl's voice sounded a little choked as she settled back down. "I spent a lot of time thinking about my name before I left the mountain. That I did have a name, but I didn't really know what it meant. Or who I was anymore, now that my head wasn't flat and I didn't look like the same person. I hadn't been allowed to think my own thoughts in so long, I had almost forgotten how. It made me sadder every day, until I just started walking away down the mountain." A quirk of a smile touched her lips. "Spider girl. Do you know, I like that. Spider Girl Landria. But is it right?"

"Right?" Reera queried, pulling one set of knitting needles out of the apron strung low on her thorax. "How do you mean, 'right'?"

"Names are something you either get from your parents when you're born, or something you take and make for yourself. Begging your pardon, Miss Spider, but you can't really give me a name that's real."

The answer pleased Reera, and she waved a foreleg. "My pardon, Landria. Do go on. Tell me your thoughts. I am, for reasons of my own, absolutely fascinated to hear them." With dexterous claws, she started working on her knitting project again, letting the purple ball of yarn roll out between the pair of them. "And you may call me Reera."

The girl's eyes flashed ever so slightly purple as she watched Reera's knitting, and she pulled a small crochet hook of her own out of a pocket, along with a wad of spider silk. "May I? Thank you, Reera. So this afternoon, I was thinking about how the spiders don't seem to have individual names. At least, that I can understand. There's a faint hissing, and some combine it with a drag of one foot or another along the ground. I'm fairly sure that's them naming one another, but I cannot quite imitate it or repeat it yet. It's so interesting when they can speak aloud. Like they have multiple languages, and only some of them I hear with my ears. But it's vibrations. I wonder if words are vibrations too."

Four of Reera's eyes blinked. "They are, of course. Words and sounds are vibrations through the air. Where do you think thunder and wind carry them from? When you speak, touch your throat and feel. All sound is merely vibration of one kind or another."

The girl's eyes widened with every word. "Yes! Yes, exactly! And I don't really have the knack of knowing which spider makes which sounds to call a specific other one, although I think my primary Dictator Spider… er, the spider I bring food for, is named something like two taps with a back leg, along with a soft three-syllable chitter. I can't make the noise right yet, and she asked me to stop trying as it was giving her a headache."

"Very good. Yes. You are thinking very useful thoughts."

Landria tilted her head. "Am I? The spiders just made a hissing laugh at me when I asked them, but I think they got just a little nicer in asking me to do things after I tried it."

"Many beings become a great deal nicer when you try to understand their perspective and speak their language. It's a most excellent habit. What else are you thinking?"

The girl made a decidedly unkind face. "Well, with the Supreme Dictator's wife doing bad magic to people, and with that fairy princess making our heads round — no one asked me if putting them in my skull was what I wanted, by the way. I mean, yes, I was most pleased to get my can of brains back. But then whoops-a-daisy, my head is suddenly weird and round and I don't have a brain can any longer. So. Can I confess that I'm also thinking some grumpy thoughts? Shouldn't someone have asked my permission before they changed what I looked like and how I thought? And where?"

Reera tilted her whole body forward intently. "Yes indeed, they should have. It is bad to transform someone who can think and talk without their express permission. I have had a lot of arguments with a very large woman on the topic over the years. Do you mind the idea of transformation in concept, or in specific application to you?"

Landria shook her head, confused. "Hm?"

"Let me try again. Do you hate the idea that someone could change your shape, or are you merely angry that someone did it without your permission?" Reera phrased her question with care.

"I have…a lot of feelings both ways," the girl said after a short pause. "I love the idea of being able to change my own shape. If a person could change themselves for the better, and hopefully not for the worse — or in a way that does anyone damage— I think that would be splendid. But to change someone else in their shape or brain without asking them, that's a lot of assumptions. That's taking responsibility for someone else's whole life and future, and I'm not sure anyone can do that for someone else.

Not and be completely good, you understand?" Finding herself restless, the girl started hooking on a chain stitch of spider silk.

Reera's tone was very dry, even for a spider. "Oh, I understand completely."

"You see, I have a theory. It's a new theory, but it's one I've been thinking about nearly constantly since I came to the spider warren."

"Tell me."

Landria grew more animated as she talked. "I call it the law of unintended consequences. And how everything you do has a reaction. You wave your hand, you get a tiny wind, right? A small hand, a small wind. Large wings, a larger wind. I bet a dragon could even make a thunderclap of wind."

"She absolutely could." Reera smiled to herself, remembering a contest with an old friend.

"So if everything you do or say has consequences, then everything you say is important. And how you say it. Because everything is listening all the time." As the girl talked, she stabbed at her crochet work, the little hook flying in and out. "And if everything you say matters, then everything you do matters too. Because it's all connected. If you plant a tree right by a fence and water it, the tree's roots grow. So if you have fence posts right under that tree that you water more than others, the roots could grow those fence posts crooked over time. It would move the posts around, forcing them to tilt out of true. Right? Consequences. How do you get mad at the tree when you made the mistake of putting it in the wrong spot? And I think that most people don't really sit around and think about all the possible consequences of what they're doing."

"They do not." Reera paused and tucked her knitting back away as she watched the girl intently. "It's why I'm not that fond of people in general. They don't think, they don't plan for long-term repercussions. They don't really listen."

Landria beamed at Reera, relief flashing across her face. "Yes. Yes! You get it! I mean, that has to be how magic itself works, right? We are all made of magic, of vibrations and intent and will and thoughts, combined with, well, solid patterns." She flapped her bit of embroidery and then pinched her own skin before going back to hooking the thread. "I haven't quite worked out how the bit that is solid reacts with the bit that is will and vibrations. I mean, I finally figured out how to talk to my tea so that it doesn't get cold. But that's just applied vibrations, right? Water boils and moves. When things vibrate, they get hot."

"Tell me, if you know, were your brains some of the ones that the, ah, Supreme Dictator's wife used?" Reera considered the memory of the witch turned pig and back again.

Landria's hook paused. Slowly, "I don't know for sure, but I think so. I remembered that she ordered me about in the palace, and then there was a day that I stopped remembering things for a while."

Reera nodded to herself. "Thought so. I believe that your thinking is special, and not at all common. Most people don't like the idea of looking at the consequences of their actions." She paused, then admitted slowly, "Sometimes my own pride runs away with me, and I do things I have not thought through to their logical conclusion."

The girl looked up at the spider, examining her from her eye cluster out to her leg claws with greater care. "Oh! I had not thought any of the spiders really bothered with long-term planning. This is why I took over how to catch and process their food. They were really inefficient, living day to day in terms of gathering food. I was thinking that if they raised earthworms and bugs and other insects, it's much easier to process them in bulk. I have changed an entire clearing back yonder to make the job easier and faster."

"As it happens, I am only temporarily a spider," Reera admitted, rubbing one slightly purple fur-covered leg along another. "I do not much care for grubs or insects. Honey and fruit, now. There's a treat."

Landria was silent for a long moment, staring at the large purple spider in front of her. Then, slowly, "I believe maybe I heard the name Reera before, in the palace. I had only just gotten my brain back, so the thought is small and I have no real concept of the meaning behind it. But I have a memory — something about how you looked human and saved the Adepts, and the new Queen?"

"This is what comes of helping people," Reera muttered, a trifle grumpy at the topic. "I would consider it a kindness if you would simply not mention it. I really do not want to help everyone who thinks they need a magical solution to a thorny problem."

The girl was swiftly on her feet. "Oh no! That would be terrible! If everyone wanted only magical solutions, then there would be no planning at all! No thought at all for all those consequences! People would just do stupid and bad things all the time!"

Reera's spider heart warmed a little for the girl, and she hastily thought cooler thoughts lest she transform into something mammalian by accident. "Well. Exactly. But it brings me to an important question. If you were the sort of girl who could figure out for herself how magic worked in the natural world, who could make things different by changing the… to use an analogy you seem already familiar with, the knots and weaving. What would you do with that knowledge and ability?"

There was a long silence at that, and the girl sat back down to ponder it. "I don't know that I'd do anything at all," she said after a moment. "I mean, I suppose I would want to experiment a little because I like understanding things and knowing what the possibilities are. I mean, possibility is another facet of consequence, isn't it?"

"That is certainly another way to look at it. But possibility has a long tail."

"Possibility becomes consequence," Landria agreed, tasting the words in her mouth. She stared at her now triple chain of crochet and wrapped it slowly around her wrist. "I don't think I'd do very much with it. I really don't know enough to make those kinds of decisions that would affect other people. But I couldn't promise that I would never, if it would save someone or take a lot of pain away. I mean, if they wanted me to help them specifically and I found out there was no long-term harm I could see in doing it."

The spider couldn't smile, but Reera's voice was a trifle gentler. "Then I can say something. And I want you to understand that it isn't to you, but only about you." She rose on all eight feet and tilted her mandibles upward. "Glinda, whenever you read this, tell Locasta I did what she asked. And I think the girl isn't going to be a threat to anyone. Leave her alone! Leave her strictly alone, and do NOT send any of your well-meaning but bumbling little detective parties to her to get help solving Ozma's problems. If you do, and I find out, we will have strong words."

The girl was staring at Reera. "I don't understand. What…who are Glinda and Locasta? And do you mean Ozma, the fairy princess we met at the Palace?"

"I do." Reera bobbed once in a spider-like nod. "Now, because you are actively interesting, which I must confess no other person has ever been for me outside of that Mrs. Yoop in our early days, I will return and we will talk again. In the meanwhile, I'm going to send you back to your duties tending to the spiders." A single claw dipped into her apron pocket and brought out a tiny bit of ashy dust. "If you desire further conversation with me, that is. I find your thoughts interesting and, unlike those of many humans, full of truths. I could explain more of what I mean, but you're not quite far enough along the path to walk right beside me. Do you want to speak again?"

"I'd like that," Landria whispered.

"Then here." Reera touched the bit of ash along the girl's neck, who bravely stood still as the claw dragged along her neck. "Just a touch. It will grow as you do." And now, tattooed on her neck, bloomed a tiny purple seed just starting to sprout a single stem with two purple leaves.

The girl's fingers felt along the bit of shimmering color now traced on her skin. "What is it?"

"A promise, with an eye for long-term consequences." Reera backed away from the girl. "With all due consideration of all the potentialities. I like you, girl. Your pardon. Landria. I will remember your name, even if you forget it in the future because of someone else." She looked upward again. "And that means ANYONE else, Glinda! My word on it."

The air shimmered very slightly as the Yookoohoo's oath spread through the air of the clearing and beyond. And when the shimmer died down, Reera turned to skitter away through the trees. "Until next time."

Landria stared after the bulky retreating form, a hand on her neck. "So very strange." She lifted a hand, astonished to feel a very faint breeze, as if the spider's words were still being whispered against her skin. She was still a long moment before feeling a more familiar sensation, a set of rhythmic vibrations on her ankle band. The spiders were ready for a meal, and she had work to do.

Something of Great Consequence had clearly happened to her. A nobody scullery maid. A girl named Landria with holes in her memory. As the girl tucked her crochet project away and turned back to her work in the spiders' version of a kitchen, her mind was already racing to identify new possibilities that might yet come. Maybe she did have a new name, if she liked it, and she was, after all, something of a new person. Spider Girl Landria sounded unique, but more importantly, it had the vibration of something that was only hers.

She was doing new and useful things for the spiders, after all. And she was thinking new things that were interesting enough that someone with a name like Reera the Red wanted to talk and listen to her about them. That was the best part.

THE STRANGE LODGER OF OZ
Patrick Barb

From the moment he'd received word that others dwelling within the green walls of the Emerald City had laid eyes upon the mysterious figure who'd taken up a room in the Royal Palace—apparently paying Princess Ozma a nominal (and, by all accounts, quite reasonable) fee for his lodgings, the Wizard decided that he did not and *would not* trust this stranger, and, indeed, was fast to suspect the lodger in question of great mischiefs and ill intentions. "You see, it's not that I'm jealous. By no means! I don't long to live in the Palace again. I did have quite a time of it, even if some may have seen fit to call me a humbug toward the end of my, *ahem*, reign. But to live there again? No, thank you," he told a group of children playing around him—each completely oblivious to the Wizard's use of the space for his out-loud musings. "No, no, no, I've had quite enough of that life, as you know."

As it stood, the children did not know, because it had been some time since the Wizard's balloon carried him aloft from the carnival grounds and landed him smack-dab in the land of Oz, certainly long before these particular youths had taken their first steps or even sucked in their first breaths of Oz-tinged air. They had no more memory of the Wizard as the shape-shifting Great and Powerful Oz than they did of their existence as a twinkle in their fathers' or mothers' eyes.

Besides, not one of them was paying the Wizard the slightest attention.

Scratching the top of his bald head until an irritated spot beamed ruby red, the Wizard set aside contemplations of his past, choosing instead to review the facts of the matter—that matter being the arrival and subsequent lodging of this stranger whose very presence irked the little gentleman something fierce.

It was night in the Emerald City when the stranger came calling. Not just that first part of night when the memory of sunlight is fresh in the minds and perhaps even still imprinted on the eyes of those hustling to wrap up their days in time for supper, fellowship, and, finally, at long last, sleep. No, this was an incident from the middle of the night, when there's no mistaking night from day. At that exact, dictionary-definition-perfect moment of the evening, a loud and fierce knocking echoed off the gates. This knocking was so sharp and discordant that it caused nearly every citizen living in the Emerald City to wake at once and say, "Now, who could that be?"

The remaining specifics varied across the tellings, at least based on the sample size taken by the Wizard. And so, either the stranger broke down the gates or had them opened for him. He either had an easy time of sweet-talking his way past the wary gatekeeper or he disarmed the man, passing through the gates and scuttling to the doors of the castle as though it belonged to him and not to the precious Princess Ozma. From there, this stranger was either given a room, took one for himself, or there was some third option that the Wizard nor anyone else he'd spoken with had thought of.

While the specifics of how and why remained elusive and ever-changing with each fresh telling of the tale, who and what appeared more concrete. At least, at first glance. This stranger wore a long dark coat, black as the night in which he'd arrived and shiny with brass buttons. Buttons, so shiny they might be mistaken for stars. This night-sky jacket was so long that its bottom brushed the ground whenever he moved. Doing so, the jacket produced a noise akin to a million fairies armed with push brooms sweeping clean the very earth on which the stranger trod. The staccato clatter of thick-soled heels punctuated this sweeping, marking the stranger's arrival and departure, as well as whatever it was he did in between those moments. *Clip clop swoosh. Clip clop swish. Clip clop swoosh.*

On and on, just like that.

When asked to describe the lodger, accounts fell to this discussion of his wardrobe. The reasons were twofold. First, because it was indeed a memorable coat, and that sound was certain to stick around once heard. *Clop clip swoosh. Clop swish clop clip.* Just like that. The second reason also had much to do with clothing choices. Because it was found that the strange lodger would only let himself be seen wearing a black stovepipe-style top hat pulled down hard against the top of his head, and with the slash of a red scarf wrapped tight around the bottom portion of his face.

This combination shadowed the man's eyes and covered his nose and mouth, shrinking the number of distinctive and recognizable facial features to zero.

Whatever citizen of the Emerald City happened to be nearby, man or woman, child or aged, bird or beast, the Wizard took them by the shoulder, turning them just so and pointing to the Palace window, where the strange lodger was always seen, staring right back out said window and down at the Wizard and whomever he'd enlisted in his observations. Black-hatted, becloaked in black and brass, red scarf around his face, the stranger *did* cut a rather chilling figure, truth be told. And when the lights of the city caught the palace just so, a shadow stretched from that occupied window. In this way, the lodger would appear ten or twenty feet tall, though a rather flattened ten or twenty feet.

"What do you suppose he's thinking? Better yet, what do you suppose he's plotting?" the Wizard asked, stroking his chin so hard that he yanked loose pieces of a beard before it could take up residence on his face.

"Let go of me," one citizen said.

"Leave me alone," said another.

"I don't have time for this."

"Don't you have anything better to do?"

"No, no," the Wizard rebuffed. "I doubt he's thinking anything like that."

Then he'd sigh and turn to address his temporarily conscripted companion. But every time, he found they'd slipped away or perhaps...been spirited away. Then, when he'd check the palace window once again, he'd find no trace of the lodger, only a cold tickle on the back of his neck, an icy-fingered inkling.

Committed to proving there was indeed foul corruption at work, connecting the strange lodger to these disappearances, the Wizard set out to take a census of those dwelling in the Palace in addition to maintaining a running tally of those who were going *poof* and *away* never to set foot outside the building again. Every morning, he resumed his post outside the Palace, tallying the comings and goings of all who dwelled within or who'd come to visit. Among this number included everyone from guards to scullery maids, to the most wise and intelligent Scarecrow, and even little Ozma herself.

The Wizard compared the numbers before and after, finding himself shocked, though not necessarily surprised, by the results. "They don't match," he said to a black cat rubbing against his leg. "People go in but don't come out."

"Meow," said the cat. She could speak but had chosen not to. If she did, she might've said, "That's not enough proof and certainly not enough to connect to this lodger with whom you've become so obsessed."

Regardless of what the cat said or did not say, the Wizard remained certain of his hypotheses. Indeed, the only person in the Palace who never seemed to leave was the cloaked stranger. He apparently showed no intention of ever departing. Whatever happened inside the palace or near the royal throne room of Ozma, this strange lodger seemed intimately tied to it—at least per the Wizard's conclusions.

How to prove it, though? he'd thought to himself. *How can I discover what this menace is doing, making those citizens disappear as it would seem very clearly he is doing?*

Having begun to learn real magic from the good witch Glinda, the Wizard pulled on both ears as he thought, trying to recall a spell that might allow him to either bring the lodger to him or bring the Wizard into the stranger's palace accommodations. Unfortunately for the Wizard, by the time he was considering such a course of action, all of the palace-dwellers, particularly those working the doors, had decided the Wizard was "making people uncomfortable," and, as such, a vote was taken to block him from entering the palace proper.

"Fiddlesticks," the Wizard said when this news was relayed. "Now I must think of a way inside the Palace. A magical way. Something light and pure, yes indeed. That's the way of it."

But, still being early in his magical studies, the Wizard could not locate the proper spell to address the problem at hand. He found many others, however: one that would let him see inside walls, but only when inside a building, and one spell whose results were not too dissimilar to whatever was inside the "powder of life" which had brought Jack Pumpkinhead to a state of living. But none of those seemed of any immediate usefulness.

Pacing back and forth across the street from the palace, he found his brainstorming moving in the direction of more unscrupulous schemings.

Holding a green glass bottle with a handkerchief soaked in spirits tucked just past its open lip, the Wizard wound up his throwing arm and pretended to hurl the concoction, bottle and all, toward one of the Palace windows. In his vest pocket, he carried a box of sulfurous matches. Long-stemmed ones that unlit looked like flowers pre-bloom, but when struck would blaze and flicker like orange tulips reaching for the sun.

"It's a simple matter," he said, thinking that he spoke only to himself. "Light the kerchief with the flowering match, toss the thing through a window, and then the fire will draw everyone out, including the stranger."

From behind the little man, there came a light and bright clearing of a throat. He turned, releasing the bottle and rag and matches all at once. But rather than striking the ground, each item was soon encased in a pinkish-whitish bubble that hovered several inches above the earth. The Wizard's eyes bulged when he saw who was behind this magic.

For it was Glinda, the Good Witch of the South. The very same good witch who'd allowed for the Wizard's return to the Emerald City after his initial self-imposed exile. It was Glinda who'd started teaching magic—*real magic*—to the Wizard. If there was anyone worse to overhear plans for property damage and deception than good Glinda, the name or rank of that individual could not be conjured by the Wizard.

"Glinda!" he exclaimed, hoping a wide, teeth-displaying smile would prove effective in deflecting any critique.

"Dear Wizard, tell me, what is this I hear of plans to set fire to the Palace—a palace where so many of your dear friends do work and live?"

The Wizard, still and perhaps always an incorrigible sort, was quick to respond. "Fire! My goodness. What a horrible idea. Imagine what might happen to that Scarecrow and all his brains. Who would ever suggest such a thing?"

"You," Glinda said, her voice still light and gay, but with something beneath suggesting that she would not tolerate further deceptions.

As such, the Wizard pivoted to a different tactic, attempting to bring the Good Witch to his side. "It's a matter of most importance that this strange lodger be exposed. I can't say for certain how I know, but I do. In my brain, my heart, down to my toes. People are going missing!"

With a nod, Glinda made the rag-and-bottle combo and the Wizard's matches all disappear. "But I can make things *and* people disappear," she said. "Are you saying that I am strange and sinister?"

The Wizard shook his head, denying this proposal. "Well, no, by no means," he said. "Yet I can see your face and hear your words and know that you are a good witch by both name and action. The lodger, meanwhile, gives no accounting of himself."

Glinda sighed, considering the Wizard's logic, which he may have considered sound, but which she identified as having several holes.

However, before she could respond and enumerate these holes, the Wizard lit upon another idea for confronting the lodger and confirming if his suspicions were correct. "Say now! Glinda, you just showed you can make things disappear, yes?"

Glinda gave the slightest nod and started to speak, but the Wizard was moving on already. "So, if you can make things and people disappear, tell me, can you also make them *appear?*"

"Appear?" Glinda said, echoing the Wizard's last word.

The former showman, former ruler, sometimes inventor, lately magic trainee, and current concerned citizen nodded fiercely. "Yes, yes," he said, doubling his affirmation. "It's a beautiful, wonderful, simple idea. I'm amazed I didn't think of it sooner. You can make this lodger appear here. Right here. Right in front of me. Then I'll ask for an accounting of his presence and his actions."

Glinda, passing her wand back and forth between her hands, appeared to consider the proposal. And, being the wise, good witch that she was, she did offer up questions. "But Wizard, my friend, what gives you the right to accuse this man?"

At that, the Wizard puffed out his chest and declared, "What gives me the right? What gives me the right? Why I will tell you...!"

However, it was at that moment that the Wizard was struck by a feeling that deflated the balloon of pride once burgeoning inside his chest. Instead, his chin quivered and his brow wrinkled. Thinking back on mischiefs in which he'd engaged before seeing the light, he hung his head, with this pitiable expression on his face.

With a face just like that, he finally said, "I know because this lodger, for whatever reason, reminds me of myself. Of the tricks and lies and deceptions I utilized in gaining power. Yet worse. Much worse. On account of these disappearances."

Satisfied, not so much by the man's words but by the pained expression of regret over past actions that he couldn't possibly hide from his face, Glinda gave a nod. And, *poof,* just like that...the strange lodger was out of the palace and out on the streets. More importantly, he now stood before the Wizard.

For all the build-up, for all the big talk and anticipation, the Wizard—miracle of miracles—found himself at a temporary loss for words.

The lodger, still wearing that scarf and coat and hat ensemble, stared right at the Wizard with eyes glowing red. Truth be told, those glowing eyes did little to dissuade the Wizard of his suspicions. "I say," said the Lodger, though his words were quite deep and grumbly and muffled by the scarf above all else so that it sounded more like "MMM MMMAY!"

For convenience's sake, we'll translate this muffled baritone speech so that readers are not stuck playing "guess the words," here, at the point of the story when things are really picking up.

"This is preposterous! Treasonous! Devious! Devilish! Can an individual not bask in the comfort of their lodgings without accusations being flung about willy-nilly?"

It was at that point that Glinda, who spoke muffled baritone quite well, gasped and then spoke. "We never said anything about accusations," she said.

With that, the Wizard clapped his hands together and began to feel somewhat closer to his old self. "That's right! We never said any such thing. Perhaps you're feeling a tad on the guilty side, sir?"

But the lodger matched the Wizard's enthusiasm with a passion all his own. "This means nothing. Nothing at all! Now, if you will excuse me, I have business back in my palace. I mean...the palace."

Hearing this slip-up, the Wizard arched an eyebrow at Glinda as if to say *Now, do you see?*

However, the lodger, who, outside of his oversized headwear, stood near equal in height to the Wizard, turned his back on the little man *and* the good witch, all set to return to his lodgings and continue whatever business he had going on within its walls. But the stranger had made the most grievous error of underestimating the quickness and nimblefingeredness of the Wizard. As the lodger turned away, the Wizard spied the mystery man's red scarf fluttering somewhat at his back. Quite fortuitous indeed for such a wind to blow at that moment!

The Wizard's hand shot up, and his fingers closed upon the end of that scarf. He held onto it as tight as he possibly could. As the lodger marched toward the palace, the scarf came unwound from his face. Round and round, until the Wizard held up the long red piece of fabric like the skin of some massive jungle snake, and the lodger's face was at last revealed to the world.

"There's two of them!"

That was the cry that rang out from the children still engaged in frolics outside the palace. Apparently, whatever was revealed when the Wizard snatched the scarf from off the lodger's visage had been enough to cause the young ones to pause their games of play and pretend.

"They look just the same!"

This second exclamation was enough to fully stoke the curiosities of both Glinda and the Wizard, such that both rushed to get ahead of the lodger and see just what had invoked such reactions.

And it did not take long for the duo to see what it was that had shocked the children so.

"There's two of you," Glinda said. And, indeed, there was, because the lodger's face bore an uncanny resemblance to that of the Wizard. He matched the man in brow, nose, chin, cheeks, ears, and almost everything. Except, of course, for his glowing red eyes.

Taken aback by this revelation, the Wizard began to feel faint. "He looks just the same," the little man said.

For his part, the lodger appeared quite confused, unsure of what to do or whether to stay or go. He seemed like a marionette; strings cut, or at least so tangled that no one could make him move, not even himself. His mouth fell open in shock, and this drop of his jaw sounded like a loud creaking.

Indeed, it was this creak that pulled everything into focus for the Wizard. The stiff movements of the lodger. The shiny veneer of his "skin." Those red glowing eyes. The way he never seemed to eat or sleep. As his conclusions were drawn about the identity of this lodger, the Wizard could only say, "Oh."

Now, Glinda recognized the weight of that "Oh" and sensed its implications. "Wizard?" she said, the one word serving as both query and demand.

With another sigh, the Wizard began his explanation. "You recall the marionette people I made? Those who could move without strings?"

Glinda nodded.

"Well, now, first I must ask, no, I must insist that you please *not* get mad at me. Certainly, don't get mad when I am a changed man now and no longer a humbug and haven't been for quite some time."

"Go on," Glinda said.

The Wizard took another deep breath and then breathed out his breathless answer. "Okay, alright, okay, so during my exile I might have possibly come to miss my time as the ruler of Oz and not thinking I would ever be in a position where I was back within the walls of the Emerald City, I maybe most certainly made a marionettic automaton almost matching me in appearance and instructed this creation to move back along the Yellow Brick Road to the Emerald City, where they were to gain access to the palace and secure it for me. This engineered double would serve in my place until I returned and we came face to mechanical face. Like now...."

"Oh. Oh my," said Glinda, taking in all that the Wizard had shared.

Of course, just as the Good Witch of the South was hearing this explanation, so too was the lodger. And the Wizard's double, realizing that he was in fact not a strange lodger at all and did not operate under his own volition, began to experience a kind of malfunction, starting from his internal mechanisms and working outward. As the red light beaming through his eyeholes increased its brightness, a thick, soupy smoke spooled out from every available opening on the Wizard's constructed double. Before either Glinda or the Wizard could do anything about it, the lodger was swallowed by a pea soup-thick fog of his own making.

"Oh no, he's gone!" Glinda declared.

But the Wizard, still clever as he'd ever been, listened for the other's sweeping jacket and boots clicking and clacking against the ground. *Swish clip clop Swoosh clip swoosh clop.* "Come, Glinda!" the Wizard cried. "Follow the *clopping* and the *swooshing*. They'll tell us where we need to go. Though I suspect we both know where that'll be."

And sure enough, stumbling their way through the unnatural fog, the witch and Wizard found themselves at the battered-down doors of the Palace. When they stepped across the threshold, Glinda waved her wand, and the smoggy clouds dissipated somewhat. Enough, at least, so that the Wizard could spot his automaton double and then cry out in a voice he hadn't used since his time ruling Oz: "STOP!"

Which is just what the lodger did. Turning slowly in his heavy-soled boots, the lodger held up his tiny hands, the tips of which were barely visible over the cuffed sleeves of his jacket. "Oh, alright, alright," the lodger/Wizard's double said. "But I've done absolutely nothing wrong."

Even Glinda the Good had to harrumph at this pronouncement. And yet the lodger stayed the course. "Go ahead, find someone to say I've done harm or ill. Go on," he said, the mechanical quality of his speech more noticeable with the scarf pulled away (and still held) by the Wizard.

Speaking of the Wizard, he and Glinda exchanged worried looks, since the Palace did indeed seem to be empty of all inhabitants other than the current trio engaged in this showdown. "Hmmm," said the little man. "He does appear to have a poi—"

But it was just before the Wizard could finish his "point" that he heard a knocking coming from somewhere nearby. "What's that?" he inquired.

"Nothing, oh nothing. Nothing at all to be sure," said the lodger in a way that highly suggested the opposite was true.

But the Wizard was already on the case. He looked behind doors, through windows, under chairs and benches, even inside a row of empty suits of armor—just in case. When he'd seemingly exhausted all possible sources for the mystery knocking, he leaned hard and heavy against one of the walls, catching his breath.

Knock knock. There it was again, coming from right behind the Wizard. At that, he turned and found the only thing behind him was...a wall.

Glinda floated over, having also picked out the source of this noise. "Now, what can that be? Let me just—"

But the Wizard's face, beaming with anxious anticipation, right in front of hers, stopped her mid-sentence. "Yes, Wizard?"

"I can do it," he said. "I know the spell to look inside walls. Please, if I may..."

And the Good Witch, quite proud of her student, truth be told, stepped aside and allowed her apprentice to work his magic—his *real* magic. Soon, transparent circles appeared on the walls, and within each circle, the duo saw hidden chambers, prison cells, and tunnels, all built within the Palace walls. And within each hideaway space, there were one, two, and sometimes up to ten inhabitants or visitors to the Palace. There were guards, maidens, cooks, chancellors, exchequers, the Scarecrow, and even Princess Ozma. Plus, many others.

Upon seeing the Princess so trapped, the Good Witch cast her own spell, a repeat of the one she'd used to draw the lodger out to the street. Except this time, she drew the lodger's prisoners out of the walls and made them reappear in the throne room. One by one, two by two, and ten by ten, until everyone was present and accounted for. "And I would know," said the Wizard to those cheering and celebrating their freedom. "After all, I've been keeping count."

Ozma and the others explained how the lodger had set up boobytraps, how he'd moved between the hidden rooms and passageways of the palace walls and snatched them all up until there was no one left but himself. "No one even knew of these hidden rooms and passages!" exclaimed the princess.

Of course, the Wizard, who had built the tunnels and chambers himself during his time as ruler, chose wisely and kept that bit of information to himself.

"Something must be done about that mechanical double of the Wizard there," declared the Scarecrow. "He must be held to account."

The Scarecrow, who served as Treasurer of Oz, was quite adept at holding things to account. But what he and many of the others were *not* adept at was keeping watch on automatons.

"He's getting away!" a scullery maid cried.

And indeed, the lodger was *clip-clop-swooshing* his way toward one of the hidden passageways. He'd already covered some ground. In fact, the Wizard quickly eyeballed and guessed that the distance was about one scarf's length away from where he stood—with a scarf.

So, using a lasso trick he'd picked up from some cowboys during his time as a traveling showman, the Wizard made a loop, twirled it around and around, and then let go.

Everyone watching gasped. It appeared the Wizard had overthrown, with his scarf-lasso missing the lodger. But the gasps would quickly turn to more cheers as the lodger's heavy-soled boot set down inside the red circle on the floor. The Wizard pulled tight, as tight as he could, and his double came crashing down.

The Wizard was slow to approach the lodger as the mechanical man lay on the floor, seemingly in stunned silence. Silence, that is, until the Wizard was close enough for his automaton double to whisper, "I'm only doing exactly as you made me."

Of course, these words struck at the very heart of the Wizard, reminding him of the humbug that he had once been. And so, he came beside the lodger and knelt, bringing the two face-to-face. "You're right," he said. "Of course. You are like me. Or, rather, you're like I *was*."

After a moment of further reflection, the Wizard gave a yip of glee. "I've got it! I've got how I can fix this!"

The lodger, still thinking like the old Wizard, hazarded a guess. "Will you reprogram me? Give me new direction?"

"Oh no," said the Wizard. "Nothing quite like that. I'm going to make you *real*. I'm going to cast this spell and make you me. Like me, I mean."

And before the lodger or anyone else could say anything to the contrary, the Wizard recited one of the only other spells he'd learned. Suddenly, he and the lodger were engulfed in a bright white light, completely enveloping them, consuming them.

Everyone else in attendance leapt back, shielding their eyes from this sudden brightness. Not even Glinda could see what was going on. Some will say they heard crying. Others will say they heard sobs. But no one really knows for sure.

All that is known is what happened after, when the bubbling white light went away. The Wizard sat alone on the palace floor.

"But...what...where...where did the other one go?" the Scarecrow asked.

The Wizard leapt to his feet and offered an explanation—a smiling-faced, full-throated explanation: "It's simple math. I am me, and he was me. But there can only be one me. Correct?"

The Scarecrow and the others all nodded weakly. The Wizard persisted. "So when he became me, there was one too many me's. And so, one of us got canceled out. Don't worry, though. I'm certain it was quite painless. Now, if you'll excuse me, there are some children outside playing games that I find quite compelling and sincerely hope to learn more about."

Not waiting for counters, the Wizard pulled his new giant coat around his body and marched out on heavy-soled boots. *Clip clop swoosh. Clip clop swish...*

Darker Oz, Only for Those with Courage

(for mature readers)

THROUGH EMERALD-COLORED GLASSES

Vincent V. Cava

The room was green. So very green. Its splotchy, paint-flecked walls looked like the restroom of a dive-bar after it ran a 2-for-1 appletini special on Ladies' Night. They sprouted from a floor that appeared to be smeared with baby poop, then traveled up to a mold-blotted ceiling to complete a sickeningly claustrophobic windowless box. An olive-colored door provided an exit, but it had been deadbolted from the outside. In the center of the room, there stood an easel, a shroud draped over it like a curtain of ivy. Its presence was alien, the only thing cared for in a room left to decay. Nails jutted out from the wall behind it, spaced evenly in a row like toy army men. Off to the left was an artist's workstation, worn and weathered, its table topped with paintbrushes and pallet knives. Those were green, too. Everything was.

Green.

GREEN.

The room was so fucking green.

Riv clawed at the shackles around his ankles. Heavy chains ran from his feet to a hook anchored to the wall, limiting his freedom to move about. He tugged at them, hoping the adrenaline coursing through his body might conjure up enough strength to break free. It wasn't a good plan. He wasn't buff or anything. He wasn't even particularly strong for an Ozite, but he wasn't particularly clever for one either, and this was the best he could come up with. His restraints didn't budge despite his herculean efforts, so after a few exhausting minutes he planted himself down on the floor and decided to go with his backup plan: praying the Emerald City Guard would rescue him.

He squinted up at the lightbulb above his head. It shone brilliantly, illuminating the room like a radiant booger dangling from the nose of God. Even though the glasses he wore were outfitted with protective lenses designed to shield his vision from the brightness and glory of the Emerald City, the light strained his eyes.

He was in a hell of a pickle. That much he knew. The trouble had started earlier that night in an alley behind his favorite watering hole. The toilet at the tavern he'd been drinking at had been clogged, and he had to go so bad he was sure his bladder was going to burst. That's why he'd slipped out the back door to find a quiet place to relieve himself. Public urination was against the law. He didn't want to break the rules, but he had no choice. It was a matter of health, for crying out loud. He'd lived his entire life by the letter of the Wizard's laws. What could go wrong if he committed one itsy-bitsy minor infraction? The answer, in short, was a lot.

Riv knew now the Wizard's laws existed for a reason. It turned out, peeing in an alley can sometimes be worse for your health than holding it. Especially when there's a maniac waiting in the shadows. When Riv dropped his fly, he'd dropped his guard too, and that had given his attacker an opportunity to creep up and clock him over the head. He was in and out of consciousness after that, so his memories were fragmented. He recalled a pair of coarse hands dragging him by his ankles through a doorway, his head thumping off steps as someone lugged him down a flight of stairs, and cold metal shackles locking around his legs. Beyond that, everything was a blur.

He hoped this had nothing to do with the rumors he'd been hearing. There'd been chatter of a blood-sucking ghoul running amok in the city. So far, it was mostly gossip—campfire tales whispered from drunken lips—but what he'd caught was chilling enough. People spoke of corpses turning up in gutters, their bodies drained of blood. The City Guard denied all claims, but Riv had noticed an uptick in security around town lately. Now he wondered if there was truth to any of it.

No.

The Wizard was too powerful to allow anything like that to happen. Certainly, he had the ability to protect his loyal, law-abiding citizens, even the ones who occasionally took a leak behind the Drunken Munchkin. If any sort of blood-sucking creature even got within sneezing distance of the city gates, the Wizard would snuff them out before any harm could come to those who lived there. Except, Riv wondered, if that was true, then why had the Wizard allowed this to happen to him?

The door cracked, and in slithered the monster who had trapped him in this viridian prison. The shadowy figure crept its way into the light, and for the first time, Riv could make out his attacker's features. The man was tall and slender. He wore an artist's smock, splattered with so many stains it looked like he'd just crawled out of the sewer. His nose was long and pointed. A tuft of bushy hair rose off his head like a broccoli floret.

Plastered across his face was a wicked grin. The sight of it sent a wave of dread through Riv, but there was something else about the man's face that was far more bizarre.

His eyes.

Like two glistening emeralds plucked from the walls of the palace itself, their gaze was piercing. Riv had never seen eyes before. Not in the Emerald City, where the Wizard had decreed that protective glasses would be fastened securely to everyone's faces at birth. Another carefully thought-out law to protect his subjects. Anyone without the special lenses shielding their eyes would be blinded by the millions of emeralds that lined the city's buildings and streets.

Riv knew Ozites had eyes, of course. He'd even seen pictures of them in official Emerald City-sanctioned anatomy books when he was in school, but looking at them in person for the first time felt wrong. It was as if he was stumbling upon a secret he wasn't supposed to know.

The man stood over him, staring as he swayed like a blade of grass caught in a gentle breeze. Anger began to swell inside Riv. Why was this happening to him? Where was the City Guard? Why didn't the barkeep fix the damn toilet? Things like this weren't supposed to happen in the Wizard's city! His frustration reached a boiling point, and he lunged at the man, but forgot about the shackles around his ankles. He fell flat on his face. By the time he recovered, that sudden surge of anger melted away. Only helplessness and despair remained. He stretched his arms out, pleading.

"Please!" he croaked. "Don't drink my blood!"

The man shot him a perplexed look, and though Riv was inexperienced reading eyes, he thought he could detect a hint of pity in them.

"Drink your blood? Why would I do that?" he said. He twirled his fingers, then curtseyed. "I'm an artist."

Now it was Riv's turn to be confused. The blood-sucking thing had made a lot of sense in his head, but it seemed as if the rumors were false.

"What do you want from me, then?"

Anything that could have been considered compassion faded quickly from the self-proclaimed artist's face. Now he wore a crocodile's grin. That air of danger had returned. He gestured towards the covered easel.

"An audience," he said.

He paused patiently after that, allowing Riv time to process his words. Had this man really kidnapped him just to show off his paintings?

"You're as mad as a box of frogs!" shouted Riv.

The artist cackled.

"I don't understand," continued Riv. "If you wanted to display your art, why not just petition the Emerald City Arts Commission? There are mechanisms in place for that kind of thing."

The artist gawked at him as if he'd just asked the stupidest question he'd ever heard. He huffed and balled his hands into fists. Veins began to pop from his temples.

"You think they'd ever greenlight my art?" he grunted. "The Emerald City Arts Commission is just another wing of the Wizard's poppycock humbuggery! They don't permit art! They produce propaganda!"

"What are you talking about?" said Riv.

"Think about it." The artist snorted. "The galleries that operate legally in the Emerald City feature nothing but paintings glorifying the Wizard and his closest sycophants. The cartoons published in the newsletters are just hideous caricatures of his political rivals. The plays, the novels, the slam-poetry-jamborees are merely excuses to numb the masses with rah-rah nationalist nonsense. It's all propaganda carefully crafted to serve the Wizard's narrative. You won't be seeing anything like that in my gallery. And besides, the way I intend for you to view it would never be authorized!"

So this was an illegal art gallery. Riv was beginning to see why the artist was operating in these conditions. The Emerald City Arts Commission had been established by the Wizard himself as the only entity that decided what sort of art was acceptable for viewing. This had never bothered Riv. He believed the Wizard was wise enough and knew what was best, but there were always those who, in their arrogance, thought differently. He'd heard about illegal galleries getting busted up by the city guard. What he hadn't heard of was artists kidnapping people and forcing them to view their work. This man had broken multiple laws. He needed to be re-educated and disciplined. Riv sucked in a breath, preparing to lecture him.

"Unauthorized self-expression is a violation of Emerald City civil code 2.1-71B—"

A hand shot out and struck Riv across the cheek. The sting once again reminded him just how unhinged the man standing before him was. A coppery taste settled on his lips, and he knew he was bleeding.

"Oh, hush up!" said the artist. He smiled, eyeing Riv's mouth, then extended a finger and wiped the blood from his lip. A peculiar look of bliss flashed across his face before he snapped those piercing green eyes back to Riv. "We're past petty crimes. Now, let's stop beating around the bush and get into it. Once upon a time…"

The artist stepped up to the easel and, keeping his eyes on Riv, jerked the covering off with a flourish, revealing a picture of Glinda, the Witch of the South. In the painting, she was lounging on a soft velvet cushion. Her bare feet were the focal point of the picture, taking up most of the canvas space. Their size was exaggerated, perhaps twice as big as the illustrations Riv had seen of her in the schoolbooks he'd studied as a lad. Her soles were dirty, as though she'd been walking around without shoes all day, and she had a lustful expression on her face that made the piece weirdly uncomfortable.

The artist glanced at the painting, then back to Riv. His face went flush before throwing himself in front of the canvas.

"That—that wasn't supposed to be in there," he stammered. "That's not part of the gallery. Let's start over."

He checked the painting stacked behind it, exhaled a sigh of relief, then removed the portrait of Glinda's feet from the easel and placed it on the ground against the wall.

"Once upon a time, there was a painter," he said, looking back to double-check if the right painting was queued up.

This one was of the artist himself. Riv could see that, for all the craziness this man demonstrated, he was still very talented. The picture was so detailed and lifelike, it almost seemed as if Riv was peering through a window. It was clear great skill had gone into this work.

In the painting, the man was standing on top of a ladder, applying a coat of paint to the side of a building. He was working on a mural of the balloon the Wizard had arrived at Oz in. One major distinction between the real-life man and his image in the painting was that in the picture, he was wearing the same protective glasses as Riv.

"Key word, painter," said the artist. "He didn't understand art. He'd never really seen it. Oh, he painted, of course. Murals, portraits, wanted posters of wicked witches, that kind of thing. It was his job to paint, but he never knew art. That was fine by him. After all, he was a loyal citizen of the Emerald City. He didn't think. The Wizard did that for him and everyone else behind the city walls. But art requires thought, you see, and the man depicted here was as thoughtless as a scarecrow sitting in a field spooking away birds. Until one day, while working on a mural on the Emerald City Commerce building, something happened that changed everything for him."

Riv once again wondered why help hadn't come. How could the Wizard allow evil like this to fester just beneath the city's surface? Wasn't he all-powerful? A sorcerer like him should be able to smite malevolent actors before…well, before they have a chance to act! Perhaps Riv was being punished. Maybe this was Wizard's way of disciplining him for peeing on that building.

The artist prattled on.

"His ladder wasn't tall enough for this project. He had to balance on the highest rung to paint the top of the mural. For days, he'd been asking his employers for a taller ladder, but they had assured him it was safe to use. He'd trusted them. His superiors had been put in place by the Wizard, who was wise and all-seeing. He wouldn't allow anyone negligent to supervise such a project. Despite the painter's fears, the Wizard's superior foresight and judgment was a reassurance he could find peace in as he worked. Until he slipped."

He hung the painting up on one of the nails behind the easel to reveal a new one that had been stacked behind it. This was a bird's eye view of the artist falling from the ladder. It was yet another masterful work. The terror exhibited on the artist's face was superb, and if the man hadn't been such a dangerous lunatic, Riv might have remarked on his exquisite technique.

He only allowed this painting to be viewed for a brief period before he removed it. Once it was taken off the easel, Riv found himself looking at yet another picture of a barefoot Glinda. The artist was also featured in this piece, lying on his stomach, face against the ground, while the Witch of the South rested her foot atop his cheek. There was a speech bubble above her head. It read: *Clean my dirty piggies.*

"Sorry," grumbled the artist. "How do these keep getting in here?"

He pulled the Glinda painting and placed it on the ground beside the other one, then leafed through the remaining canvases on the easel to make sure there were no more unexpected entries in his collection. Once he was satisfied, he stepped to the side.

"Really, I am sorry about that," said the artist. He paused, waiting for Riv to accept his apology. When it was met with only silence, he cleared his throat.

"The painter thought the fall was going to kill him."

"Did it?" asked Riv.

"What? No, obviously not. Are you not paying attention?"

"I'm sorry. I'm still thinking about the piggy thing."

"Forget the piggy thing!" shouted the artist. "The painter didn't die! Instead, something miraculous happened when he hit his head against the ground. You'll never guess what."

"He got brain damage?" asked Riv.

"No! Okay, yes, he did get brain damage. The painter did experience a very serious concussion, but that's not important."

He stepped to the side so Riv could see the next picture. They were now looking at a closeup of the glasses, broken on the ground.

"The impact caused the glasses that had been fastened around his head since he was an infant to break and come loose. Before he went unconscious, he looked upwards and saw something that stole his breath."

He removed the picture, hung it beside the others, and paused waiting for Riv to take in the new painting.

"So what? That's the sky," said Riv.

Sure enough, this was a picture of the sky from the man's vantage point after he had fallen. Riv leaned forward and stared carefully.

"What are you looking for?" asked the artist.

"I don't know," said Riv. "I thought maybe it was one of those Magic Eyes and there'd be a hidden picture of feet in the clouds."

The artist sighed.

"It's just a picture of the sky, okay? But it was unlike any sky he'd ever seen before. Or you, for that matter. Hell, there isn't an Ozite in the Emerald City who has seen the sky like this. And it has nothing to do with Glinda or Gaylette or any other woman in Oz with filthy, dirty, delicious piggies!"

Riv glanced curiously at the artist. Despite his fear of the man and his discomfort surrounding the foot stuff, he found he was starting to get sucked into the story. That sense of danger still lingered in the air, but it was slowly being overcome by intrigue. He knew it was against the law to view unsanctioned art, but he couldn't help but feel his curiosity increase with each new painting.

"What was so different about the sky?" he asked.

The artist chuckled.

"I envy your naïveté. Sometimes, I think it would be nice to see the world as simply as you do, but then I look at this painting, and I can't help but know the grass is far greener on my side of the fence." He shook his head. "Poor choice of words. The sky was different because I was seeing it for the first time as its true color. Blue."

Riv scoffed. Such a declaration was ludicrous. Blue was not a color that existed in the Emerald City. Everything and everyone was green.

From the gemstones that decorated the walls of the Wizard's palace, to the beer that had passed through his urinary tract earlier that night. Green was a sacred color, reserved for the Wizard and his subjects behind the wall. The idea of other colors existing in the city was as preposterous as the Wicked Witch of the West herself, parading down the street in her underwear.

"That's insane!" said Riv. "The sky above the Emerald City is green!"

The artist ignored his prisoner's interruptions and persisted. He removed the canvas and hung it up to uncover another. In the next picture the man's head was bandaged. He was back to wearing his glasses, but there was a sad, forlorn expression on his face.

"He was taken to the hospital," said the artist. "His glasses were then secured to his face while he was unconscious. The painter was given care and a couple days off work to mend the bump he'd taken on his head. Everything was back the way it had been before, but that didn't mean everything was alright. He couldn't stop thinking about that brief glimpse he'd caught of the sky. That sad, melancholy blue. What a tragically beautiful color. He knew if he wanted to see the sky as he had before, there was one thing that needed to be done."

The artist removed the canvas.

"He'd have to break his glasses."

In this picture, he was no longer wearing his glasses. He held them in his hand. In the other, he gripped the pair of pliers he'd used to snap them off. His eyes were sharp. They bore the same intense stare he had when he first entered the room.

The artist's confession outraged Riv. This feeling whirled together with dread, curiosity, and his sudden doubts of the Wizard's omnipotence, to create a strange concoction bubbling inside him.

"Removing your glasses is a high crime in the Emerald City," he blurted. "Punishable by imprisonment!"

The artist ignored him.

"He went up to the roof to get a view of the sky. To see it again, as he had before. To witness its blue vastness and its pillowy white clouds, but what he got was far more than he bargained for."

When he uncovered the next painting, Riv could see it featured a view of the Emerald City skyline.

"It wasn't just the sky that had changed. Everything had. Don't get me wrong. The city was still very much green, but so much of it wasn't. The people, for instance, came in all sorts of different shades of brown and pink. The birds flying overhead were purple and yellow. Even the city's jewels! Such a wide assortment of colors! All this time, he thought they were green! But no!"

The heretical claims the artist was making struck Riv with more horror than any picture of Glinda's feet ever could.

"The painter knew he could never go back after seeing that," the artist continued. "He fell to his knees in sorrow when he came to the realization that the Wizard is nothing more than a snake oil salesman! These glasses—the ones that are locked around your face—don't protect your eyes from anything. Their only purpose is to hide the true majesty of the world."

What the artist was now saying carried consequences in the Emerald City more severe than seeing the inside of a jail cell. Even the mere suggestion that the Wizard was anything other than an honest, benevolent, compassionate ruler was a crime punishable by death. And yet, there was something about his words Riv couldn't quite dispute. A logic to his derangement. Terror now gripped Riv, not because he was afraid of the artist, but because he was afraid the artist was telling the truth. It threatened to turn his whole world upside-down.

"Why?" Riv asked.

The artist sneered.

"Control. The glasses stifle individual thought. The Wizard believes there is only room for his narrative in Emerald City. Fasten glasses to everyone's faces and we'll see the city the way the Wizard wants us to see it. From there, you can swallow anything he tells you. But once you peer through the façade, you begin questioning all of his claims. Was King Pastoria truly unfit to rule? Is the Wicked Witch of the West really so wicked? Is the Wizard even a wizard at all? If he won't allow us to trust our own eyes, what makes you think there's even a hint of truth in anything he says?"

Blasphemous thoughts swept through Riv. His conscience fought hard to push back the conspiratorial ideas invading his mind, but his heart was open to them. In the next painting, the artist was in his workshop.

"This was where he became an artist, experimenting with colors. He was green around the gills when it came to mixing paint, but he found out quickly he had a knack for it. Through hard work and ingenuity, he was able to derive pigments from properties he found around town. Take food, for instance. Did you know that an eggplant isn't green? I bet you didn't. You wouldn't believe what color an orange is."

"What about apples?" asked Riv. "Are those green?"

The artist rolled his eyes.

"Sometimes," he said. "But do you know what worked best for red?"

The artist pulled off his smock. The sight caused Riv to gasp. His body was covered in scars. They ran up and down his arms, across his chest, and even over his stomach. Thick welts rose up over his skin. He grinned at Riv as he pulled a knife out of his pocket. Slowly, he ran the blade across his palm and stared at it. Blood began to trickle from his wound.

"You could say I bleed for my art."

Riv shuddered. The artist rambled on, admiring the fresh gash in his hand.

"Red is my favorite color. To me, it's everything green isn't. They're very complimentary in that way. Red fills the void that green leaves. Red is passion. Red is lust. Red is rage, but I realized fast that I couldn't just use my own if I wanted to paint with this beautiful color. I'd need to outsource."

The next series of paintings was appalling. Once again, the technique and artistry of each picture was magnificent. The subject matter, however, was the most horrible thing Riv had ever seen. It showed the artist stalking and attacking people, shackling them to the wall just as he had Riv, slicing into their flesh with his knife and draining their blood into buckets.

A loud pounding thundered from the other side of the door.

"Open up!" boomed a voice. "By order of the Emerald City Guard, you are under arrest!"

Finally, the authorities had arrived. The Wizard hadn't let Riv down after all. Shame began to stir inside him. He'd almost let this psychopath make him believe the Wizard was lying about his greatness. A second bang came from the other side of the door, this one louder than the last. It rattled the frame, splintering the wood. The guards were breaking it down with a battering ram.

"Not yet!" hissed the artist. "I'm not ready for the big reveal!"

He hurried back to his workstation, where he grabbed a pair of pliers.

Riv recoiled.

"What are you going to do with those?" he said.

"I'm going to open your eyes!" shouted the artist.

He rushed towards Riv and clamped the teeth of the pliers down directly on one of the arms of his glasses. Riv jerked back, causing them to snap off his face. Another thunderous crack shook the foundation of the room, but this time the door exploded inward. The artist flew back, and in stomped a handful of Emerald City Guards.

"You're under arrest!" announced the captain. "For kidnapping, murder, running an illegal art gallery..." He glanced at the pictures of Glinda on the floor. "And for whatever the heck this is!"

Riv opened his eyes and felt his jaw drop. His brain began to buffer. The room was different now. So very different. Hues he'd never seen before dominated his vision. The green smears and splatters along the walls and floor were now streaks of purple, swirls of blue, and splashes of orange. Pinks, reds, and yellows dazzled his sight. Without his glasses, he could see the world in all its vivid brilliance. It was beautiful. A dizzying kaleidoscope of colors, precisely as the artist said it would be, and yet it was still more intense and more mind-blowing than anything he could have ever imagined.

And then there were the paintings, themselves. Riv stared at them, awestruck by their majesty and splendor. In color, they were more alive than ever. Each canvas was a masterpiece. Each brush stroke, a technical marvel, blending hues in ways he could hardly comprehend. Even the foot stuff was gorgeous.

"I won't let you take me in!" screamed the artist. He threw Riv's glasses at a guard, who batted them away effortlessly. "I won't let you make me wear those glasses again!"

He hurled a knife towards the men next. This briefly stopped their advance, giving him time to dash to his workshop table, where he snatched up two paintbrushes.

"I'd rather be blind than see only green again!" he said.

He took the paintbrushes and lifted the un-bristled ends of them to his face.

"Stop him!" shouted one of the guards.

They hustled towards him, but the artist was too quick. Before they made it halfway across the room, he'd driven the brushes deep into his own eye sockets. The artist screeched and crumpled to his knees as blood began to leak from his face. Even though the sight was revolting, Riv couldn't help but think that the man was right about the color of blood. Red was such a bold, stunning shade.

"He's going to skewer his brain!" shouted one of the guards.

The artist's eyes were scrambled. What was left of them seeped down his cheeks like goopy red tears. The pain must have been incredible, but it did little to deter him from pushing the brushes deeper into his face. He let out a gruesome howl, then with one final push, shoved them so deep into his skull only the bristled ends were visible. There was a nauseating squish. His body went limp, then collapsed to the floor just before the guards closed the gap between them. Riv trembled. His mind was numb. Colors continued to swarm his vision as echoes of the artist's screams still rang in his ears.

The captain of the guards noticed him chained to the wall.

"Get a pair of glasses on that man before he goes blind!" he commanded.

Another guard darted over after retrieving the broken glasses, then held them to Riv's face. Once again, the world fell under a green filter. Slowly, Riv started coming down from his rainbow-colored high. He tried to convince himself that what he'd witnessed had been nothing more than a hallucination, but he couldn't quite swallow that excuse. He believed what he'd seen. His eyes didn't lie. The Wizard did. The men huddled around Riv and tended to him.

"There you go," one said to him. "Now you can see."

"Yes," he said. "Now I can see."

But deep in his heart, he knew that he'd never truly see again. Not as long as he wore those glasses.

Darker Oz, Only for Those with Courage

(for mature readers)

WONDOFFAL
Adrian Tchaikovsky

The Wizard peered past the curtain. They were still there, waiting. Of course they were still there. They'd made the journey to the Emerald City. They'd stood before the smoke and the light show and the flummery, the giant floating head of it all. They'd not run – these things never ran, but he thought the girl might have. They'd made their demands. They were waiting for the Wizard's response.

"We could perhaps," said his chief of secret police, "give them some nonsense quest, like we did before."

"I am running out of parts of Oz I can throw to the"—*lions*—"wolves," the Wizard said grimly. "Wherever we send them to, they destabilise. It's chaos out there. Every region these monsters pass through, they kill off the local leaders. It degenerates into brigands and warlords. Oz has become a wasteland."

The chief of his secret police burlesqued a glum face, because everything Munchkins did was excessive and comedic. The wizard had found it so endearing, at first. And who even knew that the Munchkins of the Emerald City *had* a secret police? Oh, they called it the Fun Time Jolliness Patrol or some such nonsense, but since he'd taken over, he'd ensured it was his secret police. Because there were bad things out in Oz and they always made their way to the Emerald City eventually.

The girl was the novel element. There hadn't been a girl before. Looking at her, the Wizard understood that she must come from America, just like him. An outsider, able to shake the foundations of Oz just as he had when he stepped into the old Wizard's pointy shoes. She looked just like some dirt-poor farm kid from Kansas, honestly. Probably she thought she was on a magical adventure, because last the Wizard saw, things had been hard in the dust belt. She was looking about brightly, wearing those glasses the police gave everyone. Being in Oz and not wearing your emerald glasses was a punishable offence. It wasn't just that it made the rather drab city seem glittering and bejewelled, but the secret police wore uniforms of a particular blue that interacted with the coloured lenses, so they could blend into the stonework. That was how the Jolliness Patrol maintained its Fun Times, probably. And the Wizard might have been a bad man as well as a bad wizard, but that was a system he'd inherited from the previous incumbent.

Her name, she'd said, was Dorothy. Just a kid from a farm, whisked to Oz by who knew what mischance. He watched her kneel down to make a fuss of her little dog. All she wanted was to go home. Had she come alone with her petition, he'd have done his level best, though the balloon experiments had gone through a lot of would-be Munchkin aviators without any results. But she hadn't come alone, and that was the problem.

The other three were new, but of a category the Wizard was more than used to. They were Men. That was how he'd begun to think of them. Not as opposed to 'women,' not inherently masculine – genderless, honestly, - but as a suffix to their construction.

They stood very still. None of them wore the glasses. The wizard wasn't even sure they saw through their eyes. At the girl's shoulder, axe slanted across its shoulder, was the Tin Man. It stood seven feet to the top of its pointy head, a humanoid form fashioned of cylindrical metal segments, long-limbed and rangy. It had two circular mirrored lenses where eyes should be, and below them was a great fixed chromium smile, appallingly wide—ear to ear, if the thing even had ears. They always smiled, the Men. That was one way you knew them. It stood with a peculiar immobility, as though it might have rusted in place, but the Wizard was grimly sure that the thing would swing that axe with a murderous speed and accuracy if provoked.

Beside it, the Straw Man was a slighter figure, its stuffed contours uneven and lopsided. Its hands were gnarled and thorny clutches of twigs, and it had been dressed in a yokel's outfit. Where had the clothes come from, given nobody in Oz was close to human size? The Wizard had an uncomfortable feeling that some hobo from the States had met his end in the strangling clutches of those hands to clothe the Straw Man's modesty. Its head was a lumpy burlap sack, on which had been sewn two bleak, dead button eyes and the broad curve of a maniac smile.

The third was the worst, honestly, winning out against stiff competition. Dorothy had introduced it as the Lion, but it stood on two legs, hunched forwards, long arms dangling. He could see the stitching and the seams. There had been a lion involved in its construction, but the beast hadn't survived the process. Like the Straw Man, it owed its shape to stuffing, and its eyes were blank glass marbles. A deft hand had slit the corners of its bestial maw, curled them upwards and fixed them in place, so that it bared its predator's dentition in a constant look of hungry glee. It was not a big cat. It was a Man made of Lion.

"What did it want, again?" he murmured to the police chief. The Tin Man, the Straw Man, they'd been after the usual, though the particulars suggested that the depredations of the Men were nearing their peak.

"Courage," the police chief said. "We think that's the liver. That's the seat of courage, traditionally."

The Wizard took a deep breath. "We should never have let them in."

"They always get in," said the police chief darkly. "Besides, it was the girl. At first, we just saw the girl. And we can't do anything to the girl. She's been blessed by a witch."

"One of the good witches," the physician said. Meaning a good witch, but not necessarily a good woman.

"Similarly, we can't really act against them right now, like we did the others," the police chief said. "Not with the girl there. In case something happens to her, and the witch's curse makes everything even worse." He waved his stumpy arms in the air the way Munchkins did when they were upset. It looked adorable.

"We're going to do this through flummery," the Wizard decided. That was, after all, what he was good at. The way he'd done his best to preserve what he'd found, here in the Man-plagued Emerald City. "Get the smoke and mirrors going."

The chief of police waddled over to the bellows. The Wizard hadn't been able to get past just how the Munchkins looked, when he first arrived. Not just small, but so rotund, with the little arms and legs. Egg people, almost, with their jolly, red-cheeked heads balanced on top. Only later had he found out what they were made for.

I am not a good man, he knew. *I am not a good wizard. But the man who came before me was a good wizard but a very bad man, and at least I can be a good protector to the Munchkins.*

Out in the audience chamber, the smoke and fire gushed and billowed, and the luminous balloon he'd painted up with scowling wizard's features bobbed into view. The girl was very impressed, trembling back from it. The three Men—Tin, Straw, Lion—just stared blankly, the only way they could.

His chosen Munchkins, the desperate, the unlucky, the criminals given a pardon in exchange for their service, crept out into the chamber, cowering away from the artificial creatures. Behind the curtain, the Wizard spoke into his tube, so his voice boomed and echoed next door.

"For the Tin Man, here is your heart," he declared, and a trembling Munchkin handed up the hastily stitched piece of tat. Real hearts weren't even that shape, and the Tin Man wouldn't be fooled, but its segmented metal fingers clicked closed on it, ripping the embroidery. The girl bobbed and smiled and seemed entirely satisfied.

"For the Scarecrow… some pins for that head to make you sharp." The thing didn't react as they shoved pins in amongst the sawdust of its head, even through the holes of its button eyes.

"For the… Lion," the Wizard shuddered, "some liquid courage." It was a bottle of his own special reserve, brought from the old country, and they poured it down the taxidermied throat past that hideous grin.

"But Dorothy," the Wizard went on, as the Munchkins waddled frantically to get clear, "your own request to go home is much more challenging, and requires you and I to have a discussion about many things. I would therefore invite you to come behind the curtain. However, you must come alone, for your companions have had their gifts already."

Dorothy looked nervously round at the three blankly grinning constructs. She actually thought of them as her friends! They made no response, just stared blankly at the wall, heedless of the hokey gifts they'd received. Not what they'd come for, after all. They weren't fooled like the girl was.

The chief of police poked his head past the curtain and gestured urgently at the girl, and Dorothy stepped nervously over and ducked past into the Wizard's presence.

She blinked, seeing him there—very much not a Munchkin, and the first actual human she must have seen since coming to Oz.

"Why," she said, "there's a man behind the curtain!"

"Pay no attention to that," the Wizard told her. "You're in dreadful danger."

"Whatever do you mean?" she asked, with almost painful innocence,

"Those…creatures you came in with," he told her.

"My friends?"

"Young lady, they are not your friends," the Wizard said. He saw the stubborn look on her face, the folded arms. She wasn't going to take his word for it. *Some kind of traumatic shock*, he thought. Transported to this madhouse of a country, and then confronted with these horrors as her only companions. "I am going to show you something," he said.

"What?" She was looking suspicious, as was her right. This was going to be painful. Honestly, the Wizard never liked seeing this himself.

"I am going to show you the cells beneath the Emerald City," he said.

She frowned. "Why do you have cells beneath your city?"

He smiled wryly. "Well, my predecessor doubtless had a lot of uses for them that we haven't continued, but *I* need them because the city has a problem that just keeps coming. We needed somewhere to put the Men."

Dorothy blinked at him. Across the room, the chief of secret police was at the eyeglass. It was a typically Munchkin construction, a series of joined brass sections with a lens at one end to peer into. It could be angled up so that the Wizard, or Dorothy, could look into it. It led, through a series of mirrors, to another glass lens far below, looking into the cells. The Wizard checked the view, and then let Dorothy take her turn peering into it. It was a grim sight.

The cells were barred, but the things behind them were restrained in various ways because mere bars would not have sufficed in most cases. He knew exactly what Dorothy would be seeing. Behind each was a humanoid shape built on some theme or of some substance. Some paced. Some rattled chains. Some beat and slobbered at the insides of glass vessels. Each was a horror, and every one of them grinned.

"In the cell to the left there is a Man of Leather," he said. "You see it?" The mummified face that had been an actual face, stretched askew across the wooden skull beneath. A patchwork of tanned hides made up its upholstered frame. "It came seeking lungs. In the cell next to it is a Man of Jelly." Viscid, greenish, undulating, constantly about to lose its humanoid shape before snapping back. Inside its glob of a head, a crescent of loose teeth bobbled, beneath two peeled and pickled eyes. It leered grotesquely from out of the bell jar it was trapped in. "It came looking for skin," the Wizard explained. He went through the others, those within the remit of the glass. The Man of Meat who came seeking kidneys, the Man of Glass collecting bones; the Man of Razors who'd begged, in a voice like a musical saw, for a face. And on, and on, the vile anatomy of their desires set against the artificiality of their construction.

"But why have you got them all locked up?" the girl asked, after she'd peered into the lens for a while. And her face had nothing but guileless sympathy for all the horrible Men. "Why can't you just give them what they want, like you did with my friends?"

He wanted to tell her they weren't her friends, but what she saw, looking on the Men, was not what any sane person saw. There'd been a story the Wizard read once, of an old knight who looked on mundane things and saw wonders. With Dorothy, the madness had gone the other way. He turned away. She was sacrosanct. It wasn't just that she was protected by a witch, but her naivety itself was a shield. She was looking at him with so much hope.

"I'm sorry," he said. "I don't think I have any way of returning you to Kansas."

"What's her dog doing?" demanded his chief of police. The Wizard turned to see the Munchkin had hinged the lens down to peer into it. "Why's her dog down in the cells?"

And indeed, the little dog hadn't come behind the curtain with her. "Why's it not with you?" the Wizard demanded.

Dorothy blinked at him, eyes suddenly brimming with tears at the suggestion she'd done something wrong. "But you said that I should be alone."

"Alone, yes," the Wizard said. "Meaning not *them*. Not the Men. But your little dog…"

"Please, sir," Dorothy said. "He isn't my dog."

The Wizard and his chief of police exchanged a look. "Then…whose dog is he?"

"He's just my friend. We met out in the country," Dorothy explained. "Like the others."

The Wizard scrambled for the lens and peered into it, seeing the little black terrier trotting between the lines of bars. It stopped before the Man made of meat, wagging its tail pertly, sniffing at the bars.

It opened up. The Wizard made a horrified gurgling sort of noise. The dog split open, and within was an orrery of sharp-toothed gears and jointed legs. They hinged out and unfolded and spread until the casing of the dog's skin, gaping like an empty suitcase, was at the centre of a cage of mechanical parts that reached out with more and more pieces until it had gripped the bars. Sawblade gears arose from still further within its innards and keened into the old iron. The basket of its myriad struts and parts had assumed a form that was approximately humanoid, cogs for eyes and the toothed curve of half a gear grinning below them. It was a Clockwork Man, a tick-tock thing crammed into the hide of some luckless mutt. They'd all been so occupied with the Lion and the Scarecrow and the Woodcutter, nobody had looked at the frisky little pup.

The bars fell away, and the Meat Man stepped out into freedom, the mismatched butcher's shop of its body rippling and clenching. The Clockwork Man had gone on to the next cell, but the Man of Meat was already stomping towards the exit.

"God," the Wizard said. "We've got to get out of here." He reeled back and collided with Dorothy. "Out!" he yelled into her face. "Nobody is safe! We caught them one at a time, and we lost a lot of Munchkins doing it, and then you arrived with *three!*" Four, though they'd not known. "And now they're all going to be freed!"

"I don't understand!" Dorothy wailed. "Why do you hate my friends? What have they done?"

"It's what they're here for!" the Wizard shouted. "A heart! A brain!"

"But you gave them——"

"That was just for you! To keep you happy. Do you think anybody else in all of Oz was fool enough to think *that* was what they came for?" he demanded. "Listen to me, girl, once upon a time there was a *real* wizard in Oz! Not this tired old shyster but a man of such power it took the witches of all eight points of the compass to put him down! So powerful that merely killing him wouldn't have kept him in the ground! So they tore out every part of him and destroyed it separately, left so little of him together you could fit it in an egg cup!" He rushed around the room, stuffing things at random into a carpet bag. "But he knew that's how they'd do him, you see. He made his plans! He's been slowly piecing himself back together, his ghost, his spirit, whatever you'd call it. He's been making his Men, to come find replacement parts. He's going to build himself anew, but he needs the Munchkins to do it." He pushed out through the curtain, then quailed back from the immobile smiles of Dorothy's three companions. A Munchkin waddled frantically past, and the Lion moved almost languidly to pluck the creature up in its jaws. The wretch waved his stumpy limbs, rotund body bulging under the pressure of those terrible blunt teeth.

"He made the Munchkins!" the Wizard yelled, skirting around the edge of the room with his bag held before him. "They're incubators! For organs! He made them to live and multiply, so that when he was ready to send out his Men, they'd be here to be harvested. I've tried to save them, I have, but the Men keep coming."

Dorothy, still with the curtain draped half over her, stared at him blankly, as though nothing of what he was saying was reaching past her ears.

With a considered motion, the Lion reached up and unseamed the squealing Munchkin it was chewing, shaking the torn body until something flopped out. The Wizard was no surgeon, but it would be a liver. A perfect healthy liver, just like every organ the Munchkins grew within them. Their sole purpose for being brought into existence. The Tin Man shouldered his axe and strode stiffly off. The Wizard saw his chief of police try to skulk away, but the thorny fingers of the Straw Man hooked him close, turning him so that the top of his head was presented to those dreadful button eyes.

Elsewhere they'd all be collecting their allocated parts. The Leather Man, the Jelly Man, the thing made of wires, the statue of animate wax. Each one an organ or a piece, that it would seal inside itself and then march off with. Somewhere, the Wizard had a slab laid out, and on it his constructed servants would reconstruct him a part at a time, until there would once again be a true wizard in Oz, and not one creature in all the land would be safe from his monstrous magic.

With the screams of the Munchkins ringing across Emerald City, the Wizard clutched his bag to him and fled, knowing it would never be far enough.

ABOUT THE AUTHORS

JENDIA GAMMON is a Nebula and three-time BSFA Awards finalist author of fantasy, science fiction, horror, and thriller novels and short stories. She is also CEO of Roaring Spring Productions, LLC and Editor-in-Chief of its publishing imprint, Stars and Sabers Publishing. She has also written under the pen name J. Dianne Dotson. Born in Southern Appalachia, Jendia now lives in Los Angeles with her family.

Jendia conducts workshops and participates in panels on creative writing for conventions such as San Diego Comic-Con and Star Wars Celebration. She holds a degree in Ecology and Evolutionary Biology. Jendia is also a science writer and an award-winning artist.
https://jendiagammon.com

ERNIE CHIARA is a writer and literary agent, representing award-winning, bestselling, and critically acclaimed authors at Fuse Literary for the past five years. He's been featured in *Writer's Digest*'s Annual Agent Roundup and is a faculty member of Writer's Digest University's online courses. When his nose isn't buried in a manuscript, you can find him browsing the stacks at his local indie bookstore for far too long or failing miserably to get his kids to laugh at his jokes.
https://erniechiara.com/

ERIC SHANOWER is the award-winning cartoonist of the graphic novel series *Age of Bronze* (Image Comics), retelling the story of the Trojan War. He's written and drawn dozens of Oz projects, including writing *New York Times* best-selling graphic novel adaptations of six of L. Frank Baum's Oz books (Marvel Comics). Shanower has illustrated for television, stage, magazines, and children's books, two of which he wrote himself. He lives in Portland, Oregon.
http://ericshanower.com/

J.R. DAWSON (she/they) is the Golden Crown award-winning, Hugo Award nominated, and Nebula Award finalist author of *The First Bright Thing*. They have had shorter works in places such as *F&SF*, *Lightspeed*, and *Uncanny*. Dawson currently lives on Dakota land in Minnesota with her loving wife. She teaches at Drexel University's MFA program for creative writing, and fills her free time with keeping her three chaotic dogs out of trouble. Her latest book, *The Lighthouse at the Edge of the World*, is a sapphic Orpheus retelling.

https://www.jrdawsonwriter.com/

HELEN GLYNN JONES writes about kissing and dragons and vampires, as well as spicy contemporary romance under the name Isadora Love. She's also had short stories appear in several anthologies and publications. Helen is also an Editorial Assistant for Stars and Sabers Publishing. She is represented by Lucienne Diver of The Knight Agency.

Born in the UK, Helen has since lived in both Australia and Canada. A few years ago she returned to her native England where, when she's not writing stories, she likes to hunt for vintage treasures, explore stone circles and watch the sky change colour. She currently lives in Hertfordshire.

https://journeytoambeth.com/

American author **DENNIS K. CROSBY** is the multi award-winning author of the bestselling Kassidy Simmons Series (*Death's Legacy*; *Death's Debt*; *Death's Despair*). Since 2020, he has published three urban fantasy novels and numerous short stories.

Dennis holds a Master of Science Degree in Forensic Psychology and a Master of Fine Arts Degree in Creative Writing. With experience in retail sales, private investigation, and social service, Dennis uses his knowledge and experience to craft compelling characters experiencing real world challenges against the backdrop of magical, supernatural, and mythological phenomena. He's been the subject of several interviews and podcasts, has been a guest speaker for writer's groups and multiple conferences, and he's been a panelist and moderator at WonderCon, Comic-Con International, and Stoker Con in San Diego, where he also served as Co-Chair.

Dennis grew up in Oak Park, Illinois, and currently makes his home in San Diego, California.

https://denniskcrosby.com/

NICOLE FIELD has been writing since they were handed a floppy disc and told how many Word documents could fit on it. They write across the spectrum of sexuality and gender identity in multiple genres, and live in Melbourne with their husband, two cats and a whole lot of books. Probably drinking right now from a bottomless cup of tea.

They can be found on Bluesky: @faerywhimsy and Wordpress:
nicolefieldwrites.wordpress.com

JEANNIE WARNER is a SFWA author living in the SF Bay area in California. She has a useless degree in musicology, a checkered career in computer security, and aspirations of world domination — those other guys keep doing it wrong. She has published many short stories in fiction, more than a few blogs on the topic of security, and wrote two 5e gaming books set in the land of Oz. She has a (short) movie credit, three finished novels, and a collection of snarky notes from a former upstairs neighbor. She plays a lot of hockey, drinks a lot of lattes, and believes yes is more fun than no.

https://www.jeanniewarner.com/

PATRICK BARB is a Bram Stoker Award Finalist author of weird, dark, and spooky tales, currently living (and trying not to freeze to death) in Saint Paul, Minnesota. His published works include the novel *Abducted*, the dark fiction collections *The Children's Horror* and *Pre-Approved for Haunting*, the novellas *The Nut House, The Big One, Turn, JK-LOL,* and *Night of the Witch-Hunter*, as well as the novelette *Helicopter Parenting in the Age of Drone Warfare*. He is the editor and publisher of the anthology *And One Day We Will Die: Strange Stories Inspired by the Music of Neutral Milk Hotel*. His 2023 short story "The Scare Groom" was selected for *Best Horror of the Year Volume 16* and he received an honorable mention for his short story "The Mommy, The Daddy, The Brother, and The Me Outside My House" in *Best Horror of the Year Volume 17*.

https://patrickbarb.com/writer

VINCENT V. CAVA is an author who specializes in the field of horror. His work has been published by Simon & Schuster, PS Publishing, Shortwave Publishing, and more. He is the co-writer and co-producer of the *Creepypasta* film (2023). Vincent has written two graphic novels, and his work has been used to promote film and television for Fox, Starz, and Crypt TV. His works are available wherever books are sold.
https://linktr.ee/vincentvenacava

ADRIAN TCHAIKOVSKY was born in Lincolnshire and studied zoology and psychology at Reading before becoming a professional author in 2007. He is a keen role-player and board gamer and is trained in stage-fighting. His literary influences include Gene Wolfe, Mervyn Peake, China Miéville, Steven Erikson, Naomi Novak, Scott Lynch and Alan Campbell.

Adrian primarily explores deep themes, such as artificial intelligence and alien awareness within epic galactic and fantastical settings.

He has a deep interest in the animal world specifically insects from his studies in Zoology and has a particular penchant for spiders.
https://adriantchaikovsky.com/

ACKNOWLEDGMENTS

Without the support of our backers, this book would not be possible. We thank the contributors of our crowdfunding campaign for their donations.

Thank you to:

John Kuo, Amy Goldschlager, Gareth L. Powell, David Perlmutter, Robert C. Young, Jodie Troutman, Chrystal O'Keefe, Justine Norton-Kertson, Deana M. Spencer, Prof. Karl Woggle-Bug Loeffler, Marcus Mébes, David Tai, Jason Flum, Louiz Hutchings, Kytyn, Imaginos Messmer, DC Hauser, Gili Bar-Hillel, Michael Mulhern, Paraskevi Oppio, Buffy Francis, Devin Ross, Gabriel Peña, Scott Cummings, Gloria Thomas, Kelly Varner, Lindsey Seegers, Meg Steen, Rick Russell, Blair B. Frodelius, T.E., Joan M. Childs, Cerise Cauthron, Jonas Karlsson, Andy Murphy, Rachel Carthy, Abraham Schroeder, Kaleigh Black, Brent Pitts, Mike Griffin, Miguel Rodrigues, Jonathan L. Howard, Paulette Kennedy, Dave M. Jones, Erika Ensign, Jared Davis, Mark R. Hunter, Druss5000, Laura Snow, Elizabeth Pugliese-Shaw, Brian Cherry, Laura Snow, Brian Beaverstock, Claudia Butschli, Marc Turel-Bitterli, Charlotte Catherine Tynes Hindkjær, Alan Wright, Kris R. Silva, Brandon Keaton, Michael A. Stackpole, Carrie Ancell, Jesse Reid, Dez Blanchfield, Janice Smith, Dan Puryear, Eric Gjovaag, Will T., Max Traver, Greg Gbur, Skylar Spiel, Rachel (Olderman) Cornette, Steve Adkins, Nic de Lisle, and Tom Jeatt.

Thanks also to:

Nicole N., Laura P., Sean D., Ashleigh G., Steven R. J., Laura R., KingMitchy, Aron T., Mark S., Tapley, Mercy L. C., Elisabeth J. H., Gareth B., James R., Agyei G., Robert R., John B., William B., Gaffin S., Timothy T., Stephanie C., Meredith M., Kristen L., Brian B., Jeb D., Susan H., Hayley K., James G., Alenadra S., Cory O., and all other donors, including in honor of Dr. Jennifer Kokai.

More from
Stars and Sabers
Publishing

A cross-genre anthology edited by authors and editors Jendia Gammon and Gareth L. Powell featuring short stories from stellar writers of science fiction, fantasy, and horror. This is the debut anthology for Stars and Sabers Publishing. Authors include Adrian Tchaikovsky, Ai Jiang, Alice James, Antony Johnston, Cynthia Pelayo, D.K. Stone, David Quantick, Dennis K. Crosby, Eugen Bacon, Gemma Amor, Greg van Eekhout, Helen Glynn Jones, J.L. Worrad, John Wiswell, Jonathan L. Howard, Kali Wallace, KC Grifant, Khan Wong, Laurel Hightower, Lizbeth Myles, Mya Duong, Paul Cornell, Pedro Iniguez, Peter McLean, Ren Hutchings, Renan Bernardo, Sarah L. Miles, Stark Holborn, and T.L. Huchu.

Publication date Feb. 11, 2025
Paperback: 979-8-9907055-0-0 / Price 19.99
Hardback: 979-8-9907055-1-7 / Price 29.99
Ebook: 979-8-9907055-2-4 / Price 9.99

AN ANTHOLOGY
OF
SHADOWS,
STARS,
AND
SABERS
EDITED BY
JENDIA GAMMON AND GARETH L. POWELL

Weaving fantasy and science fiction, Latinx themes, and traditional pulp stylings, this book collects 21 tales of outsiders, explorers, renegades, and dreamers as they navigate the mysteries and perils of the vast sandbox that is the universe.

From magic realism to military science fiction, Lovecraftian cyberpunk yarns, to swashbuckling tales in space, this collection spans the frontiers of the imagination and the vastness of the cosmos.

Publication date July 15, 2025
Paperback: 979-8-9907055-9-3 / Price 19.99
Hardback: 979-8-9914419-1-9 / Price 29.99
Ebook: 979-8-9914419-0-2 / Price 9.99

ECHOES AND EMBERS
SPECULATIVE STORIES
PEDRO INIGUEZ
Bram Stoker Award Winner

Of Enchantment, Enigma, and the Infinite is an anthology with magical themes edited by Jendia Gammon and Gareth L. Powell, featuring fantastical short stories from masters of speculative fiction.

Contributing authors include:

Ai Jiang, Alice James, Angela Sylvaine, Anne Corlett, Chris Panatier, Cynthia Pelayo, D.K. Stone, Dana Gricken, David Quantick, Dennis K. Crosby, Eddie Robson, Eliane Boey, Eugen Bacon, Guido Eekhaut, Helen Glynn Jones, Ian Green, J.L. Worrad, James Bennett, Jenny Rae Rappaport, Jonathan Maberry, Kali Wallace, KC Grifant, Khan Wong, Lili Hayward, Lizbeth Myles, Mya Duong, P.A. Cornell, Ren Hutchings, Renan Bernardo, Sarah L. Miles, and Somto Ihezue.

Publication date Aug. 5, 2025
Paperback: 979-8-9907055-3-1 / Price 19.99
Hardback: 979-8-9907055-4-8 / Price 29.99
Ebook: 979-8-9907055-5-5 / Price 9.99

AN ANTHOLOGY

OF ENCHANTMENT, ENIGMA, AND THE INFINITE

EDITED BY JENDIA GAMMON AND GARETH L. POWELL

When a precocious Guardian in Sector Z in New Inku'lulu—an elite space outpost—misuses her sound magic, the Guardians punish her by stripping away her magical ability.

Now Chant'L is exiled to Savage Mound, a sound island on planet Wiimb-ó, and grows increasingly vengeful—until she discovers that magic is inborn, never truly lost or taken. She channels energy from two spirit moons and reclaims her sound magic.

Chant'L summons the Nga'phandileh, creatures of unreality. But her magic is more than she bargained for when an uncontained trinity of the hive mind slips from unreality and brings peril to the federation of planets.

Now the Guardians in Sector Z find themselves with a massive catastrophe they must not only keep secret, but resolve.

A science fiction horror from an award-winning queen of Afro-Irreal genre bending.

A glossary of Bantu, Afrocentric and authorly-crafted words complements this genre-bending, cross-cultural novella. Something beautiful, something dark in lyrical language packed with affection, dread, anguish and hope.

Publication date September 2, 2025
Paperback: 979-8-9914419-2-6 / Price 13.99
Hardback: 979-8-9914419-4-0 / Price 19.99
Ebook: 979-8-9914419-3-3 / Price 5.99

THE
NGA'PHANDILEH
WHISPERER
A SAUÚTIVERSE NOVELLA
Eugen Bacon
Solstice, British Fantasy Award Winner & Otherwise Fellow

Stacey Kells never expected to fall out of reality when she packed her bags, got into a camper van with her two brothers and their best friend, and started travelling west. Sure, they might have said something like that—that's kind of the point of going off the grid, isn't it? But no one thought it would happen quite so literally. Then the world got real empty, and it stayed empty.

Now it's just the four of them, and a map that doesn't make sense, and miles upon miles of desert and sky and endless empty highway. They embarked on this road trip to figure out what to do with their lives—but their lives don't seem to exist anymore, and there may not be a way back home.

The Legend Liminal is a story about grief and hope, and the way we find lifelines in each other when we can't break free of the spiral of the past.

Publication date September 30, 2025
Paperback: 979-8-9914419-5-7 / Price 13.99
Ebook: 979-8-9914419-6-4 / Price 5.99

THE LEGEND LIMINAL

REN HUTCHINGS

Just beneath the hovercar lanes, in a Toronto very much like ours, sits an unassuming diner called Rocket Ray's. There, Shoeshine Boy spots the girl of his dreams—if his dreams ever got that good. No stranger to men, Cigarette Girl isn't easily impressed, but something about Shoeshine Boy tells her this one just might be worth her time.

Over steaming cups of coffee, they dream of a life just out of reach. Good-hearted Shoeshine Boy just wants to give his girl the moon, even if that means risking everything. Cigarette Girl, a grifter used to looking out for number one, finds her priorities shifting as her heart soars like the rockets in the sky.

When a well-dressed stranger enters the picture, he presents them with opportunities that put their love to the test. Will Shoeshine Boy & Cigarette Girl make each other's dreams come true, or lose each other in the process?

Publication date February 3, 2026
Paperback: 979-8-9914419-8-8 / Price 8.99
Ebook: 979-8-9914419-9-5 / Price 3.99

SHOESHINE BOY
& CIGARETTE GIRL
P.A. CORNELL
NEBULA, AURORA, & WORLD FANTASY AWARD FINALIST

When Louie met Marcie, he knew they'd be friends for the rest of their lives. But he was only half right.

What do you do when your best friend can't see you any more?

Like, literally.

And what do you do when your friend isn't there for you – because one of you isn't anywhere at all?

Imagine a Friend is a story about happiness, friendship – and being invisible to the person you love most.

Publication date March 10, 2026
Paperback: 979-8-9921668-0-4 / Price 13.99
Ebook: 979-8-9921668-2-8 / Price 5.99

DAVID QUANTICK

IMAGINE A FRIEND